Life and Death

LIFE AND DEATH: A Leyendas Novel
Copyright © 2017 Selenia Paz.

Published by Snowy Wings Publishing.
www.snowywingspublishing.com

Cover layout and typography by Qamber Kids.
Cover illustrated by Noora Murad Ali.
Interior by Key of Heart Designs.

ISBN (paperback): 978-1-946202-13-0
ISBN (hardcover): 978-1-946202-89-5

Second Edition.

A LEYENDAS NOVEL

Life and Death

SELENIA PAZ

Snowy Wings PUBLISHING

Para mi papá | For my father

Who showed me
The secret to surviving
What to throw away
And what to keep

Map

"The fear of death follows from the fear of life.
A man who lives fully is prepared to die at any time."

– Mark Twain

One

THE ROOSTERS DIDN'T CROW the day Miguel's grandfather died. That day Abuelo didn't get up at five in the morning like he always did. He didn't sip his cup of coffee; he didn't go out to feed the dog. He didn't turn on his truck or head out to feed the pigs and strays that were left on his ranch. The silence of the house, the absence of noise, was what woke Miguel. His sisters were asleep.

Miguel walked by his grandfather's room, but Abuelo was not in bed. He saw a small light coming from a crack in the front door and opened it, slowly, to prevent it from creaking. Abuelo was sitting on one of the white metal rocking chairs, rocking back and forth slowly. He never did that. He always sat perfectly still on rocking chairs. The movement, back and forth, made no noise.

Miguel shut the screen door behind him, but Abuelo didn't turn to see who it was.

"Abuelo," Miguel said, his voice soft and low.

Abuelo didn't turn. Miguel was about to place his hand on Abuelo's shoulder, but thought better of it. Startling him if he was asleep on the rocking chair might not be a good thing. Miguel walked around the rocking chair and saw that Abuelo's eyes were open, gazing into the distance. Miguel tried to find what it was that Abuelo was focusing on, but the sky was simply gray and cloudy. Rain would be coming soon. Miguel could tell from the smell of wet dirt.

Abuelo motioned for Miguel to sit down in one of the other rocking chairs. His rocking chair stopped moving as Miguel sat down. They sat in silence, watching the gray clouds become darker, watching the sunshine that was attempting to break through get pushed back by the darkness. Miguel's grandfather sighed.

He finally turned to look at Miguel.

"When I was a young boy, I walked to the field on a day just like this one. I thought I would have to spend the day pulling weeds from around the crops in the rain. But I didn't. That day the owner of the fields never came to work, never came to tell us what to work on." He paused. His breathing was very heavy and drops of sweat were beginning to dot his forehead. The mesh trucker cap he usually wore to block out the sun was positioned on top of a fence post near the end of the porch.

"Abuelo, should I bring some water?" It wasn't too hot outside. A cool breeze was beginning to blow, and it felt as if the temperature had dropped since Miguel had first come out onto the porch.

Abuelo didn't seem to hear the question. Miguel started to get up, but Abuelo continued.

"His son went missing. They never found the person that took him. He was just one month old."

Miguel lowered himself into the rocking chair again. His grandfather's eyes had a pleading look.

"I tried. We all tried. But we never found him. One night, many, many years after his son went missing, after we had almost all forgotten about the child, about all the children, I went out for a walk by the water, and she appeared to me. I looked up, and there she was. But I didn't know, I didn't know…"

He placed his head in his hands. He was sweating profusely now, drops rolling down the sides of his face and over his hands. His chest was moving forcefully up and down, a rough sound accompanying every exhale, and it seemed for a moment that the drops of water falling down his face were not just beads of sweat.

"Abuelo, you need to go inside. You need to lie down, to rest." Miguel placed his hands around his grandfather's right arm, ready to lift him up. Abuelo turned around, so quickly Miguel did not see it coming, and he grabbed Miguel's arm tightly.

"Miguel, it is almost August." His voice was so tight and high-pitched, it startled Miguel and he let his grandfather's arm go. His eyes stayed on Miguel's face, waiting for a response.

"Yes, Abuelo. It is almost August. And then I will have to go back to Texas, back to school. But I will be back soon. I always come back."

Abuelo smiled, and Miguel felt warm relief fill his heart. He smiled back. Abuelo sighed heavily, a long, drawn-out sigh that echoed in the morning.

Miguel helped his grandfather stand up and walk inside to his room. The mattress creaked with Abuelo's weight. Miguel opened the window a few inches to let in the cool breeze, hoping it would alleviate some of his grandfather's sweating. Miguel placed his hand on Abuelo's forehead.

"Abuelo, I am going to call for the doctor. I think he should come and see you."

"No, don't call the doctor. I am fine, Miguel," Abuelo said. His voice was lower now, soft and drowsy. "Miguel, I think I will sleep for a little while. If I don't get to the ranch to feed the animals, please go. Don't forget. The food is in a plastic container in the refrigerator. Warm it up for one minute, they will like it warm, now that it is getting cool…"

He was rambling. Miguel touched his forehead once more; it was still very warm. He ran to his sisters' room. Amelia was still in a deep sleep. She was so young, she could sleep through anything. Estela was sitting up on the bed. Miguel could tell she had been listening to the shuffling noises he and Abuelo had been making. Her eyes were wide and her mouth was open just a little, as if sound was trapped inside, trying to get out. She looked frozen, sitting absolutely still.

"Miguel, what happened?"

"I am going to call the doctor. Go sit next to Abuelo and tell me if anything happens."

"Anything like what?"

"I don't know, if he seems to be getting sick, or if he looks worse after a few minutes, anything. Just go and sit there please."

Estela rose and walked quickly to Abuelo's room. There was a soft creak of the mattress as she sat next to him on the bed.

Miguel walked to the living room and picked up the telephone. It was a milky cream color that reminded him of the caramel candies Abuelo liked to eat. He put his finger on the rotary dial and dialed the number for the doctor. He answered on the third ring.

"Hello?"

"Doctor, this is Miguel. Abuelo, I think he is sick. He is sweating and very warm. He was talking, but it seemed more like rambling. Could you please come to see him?"

The line was silent. Miguel looked at the phone in his hands, about to hang it up and re-dial the doctor's number when the doctor finally spoke.

"What did he say?"

"What do you mean? What did he say to me?"

"Yes, what did he tell you?"

"He told me to feed the animals, to heat up their food. He was also talking about a young child, a boy, who went missing a long time ago. Doctor, will you please—"

"I'm on my way Miguel." There was a click on the line as the doctor hung up the phone.

Abuelo was the same when Miguel walked back to his room. Estela was touching his forehead.

"Still warm, but not warmer, so that's good." She tried to smile, but Miguel could hear the tightness in her throat.

She looked at Miguel. "Do you think he is sick?"

Miguel shook his head. "I hope not. Maybe he is just getting a cold. The wind was a little cool this morning, and he was sitting on the porch…"

Estela's eyes widened a little. "How long was he outside?"

"I don't know." Miguel swallowed, a knot forming in his throat. He walked back to the window and closed it slowly, wondering if opening it had been the best idea.

The thought of calling their parents entered Miguel's mind. They had come to visit Abuelo alone this summer, while their parents had stayed behind in Houston, working.

"Do you think I should call Mom and Dad?" Miguel asked Estela.

"I don't know. Maybe we should wait and see what the doctor says, and then call. That way we will know something, at least be able to tell them if he has a cold or something like that."

Miguel nodded. There was a soft knock on the door. The doctor had a large brown leather bag with him, the letters L.D. monogrammed on both sides. He sat next to Abuelo and felt his forehead, then stood up.

"Will you give me a moment?" he asked Estela and Miguel, gesturing toward the door.

They nodded and stepped out of the room, closing the door behind them. They sat on the sofas in the living room and waited. The air felt colder now. Miguel placed his head on his hand and closed his eyes.

"Miguel, wake up!" Miguel's head slipped off of his hand

and a pain shot through his wrist. He opened his eyes and remembered.

"What happened?"

Estela motioned for Miguel to follow her. "Abuelo wants to talk to you."

The doctor was still in the room. He nodded when Miguel walked in and stepped outside with Estela, closing the door behind him.

Abuelo's eyes were open and he was no longer sweating. His breathing was calm and steady. Miguel sat down next to him.

"How do you feel, Abuelo?"

"*Bien, muy bien.*" He smiled.

He placed his fist on Miguel's palm and opened it. A small chain fell into Miguel's hand. Miguel recognized Abuelo's necklace. It held a small glass bottle with water in it and a tiny painting of the Virgen de Guadalupe on the front. A small cork kept the water inside the bottle.

Miguel looked at his grandfather. "Abuelo…"

Abuelo held up his hand. "Miguel, listen. You must—"

He began sweating again. Miguel stood up.

"Don't stop…" he started to say, his breaths coming and going faster and faster.

Miguel opened the door.

"Doctor, something is wrong."

The doctor came in and closed the door to the room, leaving Estela and Miguel in the hallway. It seemed as if no one breathed at all in those moments. It felt as if time had stopped in the house, but the breeze still came in through the open windows. Miguel hoped that maybe a rooster would crow, to break the silence, but none did. Who knew what they were all doing that morning in their coops. Maybe they sensed what was going on in the house.

The doctor opened the door. Miguel and Estela exhaled. He didn't look at them, and they knew.

"I'm so sorry. I'm so sorry." He shook his head.

Miguel and Estela went into the room. Estela picked up Abuelo's hand and Miguel touched his forehead. He was not sweating anymore.

No, this couldn't be. He couldn't be gone.

But he was. Miguel tightened his hold around the small chain Abuelo had given him. He held his tears in, forcing them deep down inside, and turned to Estela. "I am going to go call Mom and Dad now."

She nodded, still clutching Abuelo's hand. Miguel walked out and closed the door behind him. The doctor was standing near the front door, looking out onto the street. He glanced over at Miguel as he approached.

"What happened?" Miguel's voice croaked.

He shook his head. "A shock. A *susto* of sorts."

Miguel sat down next to the phone.

"Miguel…" the doctor began. He paused. "Miguel, did anything happen last night? Did he see anything? Did anything frighten him?"

Miguel couldn't really hear him. It sounded as if the doctor's voice was coming from the end of a tunnel.

"I don't know. We went to sleep, and in the morning he was on the porch. But I don't know how long he had been outside," he replied.

The doctor nodded. "Would you like me to call your parents?"

Miguel tried to reply, but nothing would come out. His voice was gone. Suddenly he was so very tired. He nodded and the doctor approached him. Miguel could hear his voice, but he couldn't tell what the doctor was saying. And suddenly it wasn't the doctor anymore. It was Abuelo, standing over Miguel in a red flannel shirt and gray pants, trying to shake him awake.

"Miguel, don't stop. Don't stop," he kept saying.

Don't stop what? Miguel wanted to ask, but no sound would come from his mouth.

Two

N ATALIA WAS THERE WHEN Miguel woke up. Her voice floated through the crack at the bottom of the door. Miguel was lying down on the bed, and for a moment everything seemed so foggy, so dream-like. And then he remembered.

But had it been a dream? Maybe he'd been in a deep sleep, maybe he had just overslept and everything was okay.

Miguel swung his legs over the bed and ran to open the door. But then he stopped. He felt the chain and the small bottle clutched in his right hand. It had not been a dream. Miguel walked back to the bed and sat down at the edge.

He sat and listened to the murmurs on the other side of the door. He placed his head in his hands, but stopped himself before he began to cry. How could this have happened? He looked at the little bottle in his hands, the small cork halfway inside. He wanted to throw it against the wall, to watch it shatter into a million pieces that could never be put back together again. He wanted to scream, to howl at the sky. But that would not change anything, and Abuelo's animals needed to be fed.

Miguel stood up again and changed into a pair of jeans, a blue flannel shirt, and yellow construction boots. He placed the small bottle in his suitcase, inside a pair of socks he had rolled up into a ball. He stood in front of the door, his hand on the doorknob, debating whether to wait a few more moments before he left the room. He closed his eyes and thought of the night before.

They had walked to the little store at the corner, the one with all of the *chicles* and the bottles of Coca-Cola. Earlier that evening, Amelia had been in the kitchen and asked Abuelo if there was any more of her chocolate cereal. He looked and looked with her and finally decided they could not go to sleep until they went to the store together and bought some more cereal.

They took Abuelo's shaggy dog, Conde, with them on a long rope leash that he didn't really need. He was getting so old, he would walk beside them without ever complaining. Estela and Miguel had waited outside while Abuelo and

Amelia went inside the little store to buy the cereal. Conde sat down by the door to wait, panting slightly. He had pawed at the door a few times, wanting to be let in, to see all the beautiful sweets inside. He had always been curious.

Miguel had watched Conde for a long time while they waited. His fur had changed colors, it seemed, over the years. Whereas before his coat had once been a mix of yellow and brown, now it was dark gray, and in some parts it was almost black. His chin was covered in white hairs. Miguel had not noticed he had so many. When had that happened?

Conde lifted his nose and it moved in every direction. The hair on his back had risen, slightly. He looked left and right, in all directions. The screen door creaked open and Amelia bounced out. Conde's tail began to wag and he stood, ready for the walk back. Abuelo reached down and grabbed the rope, his soft shoes shuffling on the concrete. His eyes smiled as Amelia clutched her chocolate cereal, laughing.

Miguel's thoughts shifted. They'd been in the kitchen one night and Abuelo was helping them make chocolate milk. He always put so much chocolate syrup in the milk, making it delicious and very sweet. On that night, there had been a bug flying around, and Amelia had taken the roach poison and sprayed it just as it was flying over the cups of chocolate milk.

"Amelia!" Estela had yelled. "Look what you did. Now we won't be able to drink the chocolate milk!"

Amelia's triumphant smile vanished along with the life of the fly as it fell to the floor. Abuelo was looking at her from the corner of his eye as he threw the bottle of chocolate syrup into the trash. There was no more.

He turned around and grabbed his cup.

"Nonsense! There is nothing wrong with this milk. Nothing will happen. Watch." He had picked up the cup and did not even hesitate before drinking all the milk inside. He had closed his eyes, enjoying every last bit of it. "Mmm-mmm. This is the best chocolate milk in the whole world."

Amelia had smiled and hugged him. Miguel had waited until everyone had left the kitchen before drinking his milk. He could still smell the roach spray on top of the milk, and had not been able to sleep the whole night. But Abuelo had been right. Nothing had happened.

A soft knock on the door brought Miguel back from his thoughts.

"Miguel?" The doctor's voice was soft and tired.

Miguel waited a few moments before answering, afraid his voice would betray his emotions.

"Yes?"

"May I come in?" the doctor asked.

"Yes." That was all he could say. He was afraid to say any more.

The doctor's coat had a little bit of dirt on it, and his face looked tired and red. Miguel had forgotten how long he had known Abuelo, how long they had been friends.

"Miguel…" He paused. "I have called your parents. They are on their way. They should be here in a few hours. I have made preparations for tomorrow. Are you…will you be okay?"

Miguel nodded. "I have to go to the ranch, to feed the pigs and the other animals."

The doctor opened his mouth to reply, but then closed it.

"Yes. Keeping busy right now is a good idea." He looked at Miguel intently. "Miguel, I'm so sorry." The doctor's words were so heavy, Miguel looked up to meet his eyes; but he turned away and was already stepping back into the hallway.

Miguel followed, and as they walked into the living room, Natalia rose from her chair. Miguel smiled slightly and waved. She had a box of chocolates in her hand, probably from her parents. They were always sending Abuelo chocolates, and he would share them even though he would say he probably should not be eating them at his age. Natalia's little brother Benjamín sat next to Amelia. He always accompanied Natalia, if only to play with Amelia and eat chocolates with her and Abuelo. He looked at Miguel sadly.

"I'm going to go feed the animals at the ranch," Miguel said softly.

Estela looked up at Miguel and half-stood, as if she wanted to come along too. He knew how she felt. She did not want to be home any more than he did when their parents arrived. The next few days were going to be made even worse by their arguments and their fights.

Miguel wasn't sure if Estela knew how much he wanted to be alone, but she sat down again and nodded. He walked to the kitchen and took out the packs of wrapped meat and chicken and other leftovers Abuelo would always pack together neatly for the animals. He also took out a large piece of chicken and a few bones for Conde, set down the bowl of food for the ranch animals, and walked outside to the back part of the yard. He couldn't see Conde, so he whistled low and soft. Conde still did not come. Miguel's throat tightened. What would happen when he realized Abuelo was not there anymore? Miguel walked around the yard and finally found Conde near the very back, by the tall concrete wall. He filled one of the dog's bowls with water and placed his food in a second bowl.

Conde's ears twitched as he heard Miguel approach, but

he did not turn. He simply stared at the wall, not even blinking. The fur on his back was up, like it had been the night before. A low growl came from deep inside his throat.

"Conde," Miguel said. Conde turned to look at Miguel as he set the bowl down by his paws. He sniffed at the food and licked his nose, but returned to staring at the wall. Miguel sat down and began to peel the chicken, feeding Conde small pieces at a time. When only the bones were left, Miguel stood and kissed Conde on the head and walked back toward the house. He threw the bones over the concrete wall and walked on—not noticing that the sound of the bones hitting the ground never came.

Conde growled once more.

The ranch was almost three miles from the house. The dirt road that led to it was filled with rocks that made Miguel's feet stumble.

Miguel had seen the big red barns in the picture books in Texas when he was growing up, but Abuelo never had anything like that. He had a few stables that housed the pigs and their piglets, and some small wood sheds that were home to stray cats and dogs. There were bowls everywhere, bowls Abuelo had always rinsed and filled with new water. Miguel rinsed these out now and started cutting up the meat and the chicken. The animals approached him slowly, and he made sure not to make sudden movements that would scare them away. When they were finished eating, Miguel rinsed the bowls again and filled them with clean water. He began to walk around, picking up sticks and rocks and piling them together. He cleaned the pig stables and replaced the straw with clean straw from one of the sheds. Cats and dogs came as they pleased, but mostly they stayed in the shade of the trees and the sheds.

When the sun began to dip Miguel emptied and then refilled the water bowls again. The animals were settling down on the soft straw. The piglets piled on top of each other like puppies. Miguel carried the empty food bowl with him as he walked back to Abuelo's house. He could see the tall trees surrounding the house from about a mile away. He walked slowly, the dirt and rocks crunching underneath his feet. There was a white car in the driveway, meaning his parents had arrived. His sisters and Natalia and Benjamín were on the porch, each sitting on a rocking chair. Abuelo's chair was empty, still in the same spot it had been that morning.

Estela gave Miguel a wary look. He thought, for a moment, about turning around and walking back to the ranch. He could hear his parent's voices inside, elevating every so often. *What could they be arguing about?* he thought. *Why now?*

Natalia smiled and offered him a chocolate. He sat down

at the edge of the porch and unwrapped it carefully.

"It has caramel inside," she said softly. Abuelo's favorite.

There were footsteps coming toward the front door. Miguel chewed slowly. His dad pushed the screen door open and strode across the porch, down the driveway, got into the car, and drove away.

Miguel stood and walked inside. His mother was in the kitchen; napkins littered the tabletop. She didn't look up as Miguel headed toward the sink to wash the food container.

"We will be leaving tomorrow, after the funeral," she said.

Miguel started to open his mouth—to ask what was going to happen to Abuelo's house, to Conde, to his ranch and all the animals there.

"The doctor has agreed to watch over the house and everything here until one of us can come back," she answered Miguel's unspoken thoughts.

I could come back. I could stay, Miguel thought.

He dried the container and looked out the back window. Conde was sitting in the same spot he had been that morning. His ears were pointed and, even from this distance, Miguel could see the hair on his back standing up. Miguel opened the refrigerator and took out another small package wrapped in white paper. The meat inside was soft, and he peeled it apart. As Miguel walked toward Conde, the dog's ears moved slightly, assessing the footsteps of whoever was approaching him. Miguel gave him the meat strip by strip.

Perhaps if I move slowly, time will slow down with me, Miguel thought. Perhaps it would even turn back.

Natalia and Benjamín were standing near the front gate when Miguel got back.

"I am so sorry, Miguel. My mom and I—and Benjamín—we cannot believe it. My grandparents wanted me to tell you they will watch over the house too, and over Conde. I am so sorry." She stepped forward and hugged Miguel gently. She and Benjamín waved goodbye as they walked down the street to their grandparents' home. Miguel had forgotten to tell her that he would be leaving early, but there was always tomorrow.

The windows were open in Miguel's room that night. He could hear Estela whispering to Amelia, things about the sky and the heavens and being happy; he heard his mother moving around in Abuelo's room. His father still had not returned. Conde had finally left his post and his soft padded feet would pass by the window every few minutes. Miguel could hear him as he began to run back and forth, reaching the end of the front yard and then turning back, to the end of the backyard. He ran around the house, over and over.

The house grew silent and still. The last thing Miguel

heard before drifting off to sleep was Conde's low growl as he ran toward the back of the yard once more.

∽

The wail pierced the night. Miguel sat up straight in bed, sure that it was his mother, that his father must have returned. He threw the blanket off and ran to the hall, to Abuelo's room. The front door was open—only the screen door was shut—to let the hot air out. Abuelo's door was open as well, and Miguel's mother lay there, sleeping. He looked outside. His father was still not home, and there was no one outside.

Conde was standing near the back wall, so still it seemed as if he was a garden statue, a decoration. Miguel's head ached and he rubbed his temple. He shook his head. It must have been someone else, he decided finally. Someone nearby, having an argument. Yes, that had to have been it.

Miguel went back to bed and lay there, waiting, but sleep never came. The rooster did not crow that morning, either. Eventually he heard footsteps outside, and a loud rapping on the screen door.

It was Natalia. Her hair was tangled and her clothes were wrinkled and muddy. She was not wearing any shoes.

"Miguel, it's Benjamín. He's gone!"

Three

T HEY LOOKED EVERYWHERE THAT morning. They went as far as Abuelo's ranch, and even farther, to where there were no more buildings, just the trees and the dust and the wind. Benjamín was nowhere to be found. His shoes were still near his bed, and the windows were closed, from the inside.

Natalia's grandparents came by to apologize for not being able to attend Abuelo's funeral, but of course everyone understood. Benjamín had to be found, and Miguel promised that they would continue to help them search after the service.

Amelia cried softly as Estela held her. Miguel waited until everyone had gone to see Abuelo before he

approached the casket. Miguel looked down at his
grandfather in his soft shirt, his eyes closed. Lying in the
casket, Abuelo looked different without his chain. Miguel
wondered if he should have placed it around his neck. It
belonged with him. As Miguel looked at Abuelo's worn,
sunburned face, he noticed the bushy, brown-grey eyebrows
and the crinkles at the corners of his eyes. Miguel closed his
eyes, straining to hear Abuelo's hearty laugh, the laugh that
sounded like the crackling of a fire. Abuelo's eyebrows were
furrowed, almost as if he knew that Benjamín was missing
and was wondering why everyone was standing around,
murmuring and wasting time.

The sky rumbled as Abuelo's casket was lowered into the
ground. Miguel's throat felt tight and dry, and he hoped that
no one would ask him anything, forcing him to talk. He
picked Amelia up and held her as she tied a small wind
chime to the tree near Abuelo's grave. It was their
grandfather's favorite: a small wooden house Amelia had
colored with all the paints she could find. Underneath it
hung small bells and tiny clear crystal rocks that made a soft
tac sound when the wind blew them together.

Miguel's parents agreed that they should stay one more
night, to help look for Benjamín.

"Maybe he ran away," someone had suggested at the
cemetery. "You know how kids are."

The doctor had looked over at Miguel. "I don't think he ran away," was his reply. It seemed, for a moment, as if he was certain. Benjamín did not run away.

That evening they were packing their suitcases with their belongings when there was a knock at the door. Miguel sat on a rocking chair next to Natalia.

"We are going to keep looking. He has to be here," she said to him. She looked at Miguel and waited. She wanted Miguel to tell her that, yes, Benjamín was here somewhere. So he did.

"Don't worry, Natalia. He is here, I am sure of it. He has to be nearby."

"I will see you in a week, Miguel. Benjamín and I will," Natalia whispered. She tried to smile before walking down the street to her grandparents' home. Miguel could see her head moving to the left and the right in the night, searching.

They awoke early, before the sun was up. Miguel knew the roosters would not crow. The ride was bumpy and their parents yelled back and forth, about how much they had to do when they got back, about what Miguel and his sisters needed to do at home while they were at work. Miguel knew that they were trying to distract themselves from what had happened, but why in such an ugly way? Why not sit in silence and let everyone have their own thoughts?

Miguel's thoughts wandered to Conde, who had still

been sitting near the back wall when Miguel had said goodbye. He'd fed Conde chicken piece by piece, and Conde had looked at Miguel longer this time. Miguel hugged him and the dog placed his head gently on his shoulder. Miguel's tears touched his fur, and Conde moved his head back and licked Miguel's face.

He held Conde for a few more moments. "I will be back, Conde. Don't worry. I'll bring you home with me."

Conde had placed his paw on Miguel's knee and then Miguel had walked away. Conde didn't move from his spot.

৯৲৩

Estela and Miguel spent the next few days back home cleaning the house and the yard, letting Amelia help them to help her forget. The days dragged on, getting closer and closer to the week deadline Natalia had set for her return from Mexico with Benjamín.

The Sunday before school began, Miguel knew Natalia was finally home, but was afraid to call, to visit and to find that Benjamín was not there. Miguel lay in his room that night, wondering how a person could go through day after day without really feeling it, without really knowing whether they were alive or not.

There was a tap on his window late in the night. Miguel

turned over. Another tap, louder this time. He got out of bed and went to the window. A shadow was moving around outside. He opened the window. It was Natalia. Miguel popped the window screen off and jumped out. Natalia's hair was tangled, and her clothes were rumpled again. Her eyes were red and wide.

"Miguel." Her voice was shaking.

"What happened?" Miguel asked, stepping closer.

"Miguel, I know what happened. I know who took Benjamín."

Miguel's heart sank. Benjamín had not been found. He looked away. Of course, a part of him had known that. If he had been found, Natalia would have come over with her little brother hanging on to her to show them all that they had found him.

"I know who took him," Natalia repeated.

His mouth went dry. "Who?"

"It was La Llorona."

La Llorona

THE WEEPING WOMAN

SHE WAS THE MOST BEAUTIFUL woman in the village. Maria was her name, and although her clothes were sometimes torn and worn because her family did not have much money, her beauty made them appear as if they were shining. No other woman wanted to stand next to her, to be compared. As Maria grew older and began to notice the admiring glances of the gentlemen of the village, she became more and more aware of her own beauty. She watched her parents labor every day only to make enough money for basic necessities, and she decided to use her beauty to find a gentleman who would help them rise from their misery.

It just so happened that one day a gentleman from a neighboring village was passing through on his horse, and he stopped at the village square for a rest. Maria was there, selling cloth that she and her mother had worked hard to make. Maria noticed the girls of the village were gathered around the man, some of them whispering, while others were laughing. She could hear them asking him to tell them stories of his travels. She moved closer to get a better look, and in that moment the man looked over at her. He wore a black suit and matching sombrero with black and silver boots, and his horse's hair was braided with fine black ribbons. This man, she thought, must be very well off.

She quickly looked back at her many cloth pieces and did not look up again. A shadow soon blocked out the sun, and she looked up slowly. It was him. He smiled at her and bowed, ignoring all the girls around him. She smiled, but not too much. He asked about her cloths, asked her how much they were. She sold him a few and he packed them with the rest of the items his horse carried.

He decided to stay a few more days in the village, and soon there were whispers that he had stayed for Maria. He came to see her as soon as she began selling her cloths in the morning, and did not leave until she was packing up to return home.

Soon Maria knew that he had quite a large sum of money, and horses and cows and pigs on a large hacienda. He began to ask Maria to accompany him on a walk, but she knew better. It took a few days, but he finally asked if he could court her, and she said yes. Her parents were very happy for her, and the news spread quickly through the village. But Maria continued to wait, only giving him one kiss until she obtained what she wanted most from him: a proposal of marriage. Soon Maria had traveled back with her new husband to their hacienda, and she sent her parents money whenever she could.

They lived together happily for three years, and had three children during that time: two boys and a girl. Maria could see that they were going to grow up to be beautiful children, and she was very proud. But her husband was growing restless. Soon Maria found out why he so loved to travel, why he was away from their hacienda so often. Rumors began to travel back to her, and one day while she was walking near a river by their hacienda with her children, she saw him riding his horse—and he was not alone. A lovely woman with fine golden hair was holding on to him as they rode together. Maria was heartbroken, for although she had planned to marry well to help her family, she had fallen in love with him, and with their children.

All she could see now, however, was him and his new lover, laughing and holding each other. In that moment she broke, their faces surrounding her, pointing and laughing. Her fine clothes melted away, revealing the rough cloth she wore before she was married. They stood before her, and she let out a howl as she pushed them into the river. By the time she realized it had been her children she'd pushed into the rushing water, it was already carrying them away. She hurried into the water and tried to reach them, but she could not fight the current. She could not swim back, either, and the water slowly dragged her down to join her children in death.

But even then she did not find peace. She never found her children, and was cursed to roam the waters of the earth, crying out for them, wailing, *"mis hijos!"*

...And taking any who happened to cross her path in the dark of night.

four

BEFORE, MIGUEL WOULD HAVE laughed, but the horror he felt knowing that Natalia was serious did not allow for it. He stayed silent. What could he say? Natalia looked at him, waiting, but still Miguel said nothing.

Images flashed in and out of his mind. His grandfather's house. Conde. The doctor. Benjamín. La Llorona. The Weeping Woman. A small fire his grandfather had built, years ago when Amelia was still a baby.

"She wears a torn white dress," Abuelo had said, all those years ago, "tattered at the bottom with holes everywhere. Her eyes are missing—in their place are only hollow sockets. Her hair is wet and limp, and she is pale, a frown forever drawn on her face. They say when you see her, there is no point in trying to run. She will leap after you, almost fly. She will grab you and pull you into the water to join her in her search for her missing children. And that is the last anyone will hear from you."

Abuelo had grown silent. The fire crackled and Miguel inhaled, enjoying the smell of the burning sticks. Estela gripped his hand, and Miguel laughed.

"What is so funny?" his grandfather had asked.

Miguel's smile faded, but only a little. "Estela is afraid," he answered, pointing to Estela's face.

"And what's wrong with that?" Abuelo asked.

"Yeah, what's wrong with that? You wouldn't be laughing if you saw her," Estela said, pulling her hand away.

Miguel couldn't help himself. "But I wouldn't see her. It's a *leyenda*, Estela. A folktale. It's not real."

Estela looked at Abuelo. He was looking up at the sky, the stars clear and shining. "This legend—every legend—has some truth, Miguel," he said quietly.

Then he added, a little more loudly, "In this case, you can be sure that it would be wise not to stray out of doors at night, especially near the canal in the back." He winked at Estela, who laughed at Miguel.

Miguel had looked toward the backyard at the grey concrete block wall. *Superstitions,* he thought, shaking his head.

"Please, Miguel," Natalia whispered now. Miguel opened his eyes; he had not realized they were closed. Natalia's face seemed darker, and Miguel looked up to find the moon obscured slightly by the clouds. He waited.

"Please come with me. We have to find him," Natalia said, desperation in her voice.

"Come with you? To Mexico?" Miguel asked, looking down at the ground.

"Yes. To Mexico. To our street. To the canal behind your grandfather's house," she answered quickly, glancing around. Everything was quiet. His family was asleep. "That's where she took him. I thought—I thought at first it was a fight. An argument. But you must have heard it. You must have heard the wail." She choked over the words.

"The wail?" Miguel repeated.

"That night, after your grandfather passed. I heard a woman scream, but I didn't think anything of it. A fight, I thought. A crazy drunken woman. I turned over and did not even check if Benjamín was still in bed."

Miguel looked up quickly, his eyes widening.

Natalia gasped. "You did hear it."

"Natalia—" he started.

"You did. You heard it! It was her, I know it was. We just have to find her and get him back. Tell her Benjamín is not her son…"

"Natalia," Miguel said, more forcefully this time. He bit his bottom lip. "Natalia, that is not possible. La Llorona is not real."

"Miguel." Her voice was strangled, tears building up in her eyes. "Please."

Miguel looked at her face and thought about his grandfather. Abuelo would have gone. He would have followed Natalia to find Benjamín. And if she thought La Llorona took him, he would have believed her.

Miguel couldn't believe—but he could follow.

He sighed. "Come back before daylight. Pack some things, and I will do the same. We can take the bus."

She smiled a sad smile and nodded, turning and running towards her house. Miguel stayed, staring after her, until her back blended into the night.

Any hope of finding Benjamín seemed to disappear into the night with her.

five

M IGUEL SLID THE WINDOW down quietly and closed the curtains. He reached under the bed and pulled out his grey backpack. Not much would fit, so he would have to be very careful in selecting the items to fill it. Two changes of clothing, a bottle of water, some crackers, and his wallet. Miguel lifted up the mattress and took out the bills he had saved from washing cars and mowing lawns. Almost eight hundred dollars. Enough for two tickets to Mexico, with a few hundred left over. Miguel considered waking his mom up to tell her where he was going, but he pulled out a pen and paper instead.

"Gone to Mexico to help Natalia find Benjamín."

The pen hovered over the paper for a few moments.

There was a small knock at the door. He closed his eyes tightly. Another knock.

The door creaked slightly when he opened it. Estela. Of course. Not everyone in the house had been asleep.

She stepped inside and closed the door slowly behind her, raising her eyebrows.

Miguel sat down on the bed and waited for her to say something. She looked around the room, her eyes lingering on the backpack. Her eyes shone with longing, but Miguel knew she wouldn't leave Amelia.

"How long do you think you'll be gone?" she asked finally.

"I don't know. A few days, maybe. Hopefully," Miguel replied.

"Do you—Do you think you'll find him?"

Miguel stayed silent for a few moments. "I hope so."

"Miguel…" She hesitated. "Do you really think… do you think…" Her voice trailed off.

"That La Llorona took Benjamín?" Miguel looked down at the floor, not wanting to answer. "Estela, I don't know what happened to Benjamín. Maybe no one took him. Maybe he wandered off," he replied quietly.

"Do you think he's okay?" she asked.

Miguel felt irritated. *How am I supposed to know?* he wanted to snap. He just wanted everything to go away, everyone to leave him alone. He could already envision the hours ahead of him on the bus, in the heat, and who knew how many days more in search of a fabled specter. Miguel clenched his teeth.

"I hope so," he said at last.

Estela held out her hand and grasped his. He resisted the urge to pull away. Holding hands and giving hugs was not something they did in their family. Then Miguel felt something drop into the palm of his hand—a cool chain and a small bottle.

"I found it in the bathroom. You must have taken it out of your pocket and placed it on the counter."

Abuelo's necklace. The bottle was still more than half full of water. Estela pulled her hand away. Miguel looked up at her face and saw the tears in her eyes. She stood up straight, wiped her eyes, and walked toward the door. Crying was not something they did either.

"You better go before the sun comes up. Good luck, Miguel. Be careful." She opened the door, stepped into the hallway, and shut it gently behind her. Miguel took out a pair of socks from his backpack and tucked the necklace safely inside them. Just as he finished scribbling down a few words on the note he was leaving, there was a small tap on the window. Natalia.

Miguel pulled his backpack onto his shoulder and

carefully slid out the window. Natalia gave a small smile in greeting and they both hurried down the street.

It was a few blocks to the nearest bus station, and Miguel hoped they still had space on the next bus to Matamoros. From there, maybe they could contact one of Abuelo's friends to pick them up and drive them to Abuelo's house.

They got to the Harrisburg bus station a little after seven, just in time to buy two tickets for the 8:00 a.m. bus and grab a coffee from the *El Canto del Gallo* bakery nearby. Not too many people were traveling, probably because school was starting that day. People had made their way back from their vacations and were busy getting ready for the new school year. Natalia and Miguel were supposed to be on their way to the ninth grade, but instead were choosing two seats near the back of a bus to Mexico: Natalia next to the aisle, and Miguel in the window seat.

Natalia clutched her backpack and remained quiet. When at last the bus started up and got moving, she let out a small sigh of relief. For every one of the next eight hours, Miguel knew she would feel closer and closer to Benjamín.

As the bus finally made it out of the city, Miguel began to feel more and more like a fool. What was he thinking? What were *they* thinking? How could he have followed Natalia to Mexico without trying to convince her that there was no way La Llorona had taken Benjamín? His disappearance had affected her ability to think clearly, and now they were on their way to search for him without having the slightest clue as to where he might have gone.

Miguel's heart began to beat more quickly as he started panicking. What if they ran out of money? What if they had to stay longer than a few days? Truly, Miguel had not considered the possibility that Natalia would want to stay *until* she found Benjamín. What if they failed to find him? And Mexico itself was not always a safe place to visit. That truth had never crossed his mind, and now it was too late.

Miguel thought about the note he had left. "Gone to Mexico to help Natalia look for Benjamín. I'm sorry."

I'm sorry. He could not bring himself to write "Love, Miguel," or "I love you.," or anything of the kind. Instead, he wrote he was sorry. Sorry for leaving Amelia and Estela; sorry for leaving his mother to deal with his father's anger; sorry for missing school right from the beginning. But there was another reason, one which Miguel was deeply ashamed of. He was sorry for leaving everything for the chance to return to Mexico. To his grandfather's house. To his grave.

And, he admitted to himself, as they finally left the buildings and the traffic of Houston behind, that he would have done anything for Natalia to be right. He would have done anything for the possibility of there being specters in this world—because maybe that meant he could see his grandfather again.

Miguel laughed softly to himself. What a fool.

"What?" Natalia asked. Miguel looked over at her. In the sunlight streaming through the windows, he could clearly see the dark shadows under her eyes, and the small veins around her pupils, red and pronounced. Her cheeks looked purple. Hollow. He noticed she was clutching a small paper in her hands under her backpack, and as she tucked it back into a pocket on the front, he realized it was a picture of Benjamín.

Miguel shook his head.

She smiled sadly. "I know. It's crazy, right?"

Miguel looked at her but didn't smile back.

"But it was her. I know it was," she added. She sounded so sure.

Miguel nodded and laid his head back on the seat.

"Miguel?"

"Hm?"

"Thanks for coming. You're a good friend," she said, shifting in her seat. There was a long ride ahead of them.

Miguel couldn't reply. He couldn't say anything in response to her kindness, not when—if he really considered the situation—he did not expect them to find Benjamín so easily. And not when, if he was truly honest with himself, he just wanted to run away to his grandfather's house and never come back.

Six

MIGUEL OPENED HIS EYES. The bus was still in line at the checkpoint to cross into Mexico. He looked at his watch; almost four o'clock. The way the line was moving, with any luck they would be past the checkpoint by four-thirty. Miguel had been trying to sleep throughout the trip without success, and though there were shades covering the windows, the sunlight still broke through. Even when his eyes were closed, he could feel the brightness on his eyelids. He finally resolved to alternate opening and closing his eyes, but he had felt every minute of the ride.

Natalia, meanwhile, had managed to fall asleep, and he was grateful for that. Miguel didn't know how long she had gone without rest, but he was sure it had probably been several days. Throughout the ride he'd begun to notice small things about her: the small stains of dirt on her clothing, her thin fingers clutching her backpack, her hair tangled and disheveled. He had considered telling her that it was silly to think that a legend their parents used to scare them into being good had taken Benjamín, and was resolved to tell her as soon as she woke up. As the ride went on, though, he thought about Amelia, and what he would do if she had gone missing. He couldn't imagine how Natalia was still functioning. When she finally woke up, he found he could not bring himself to do it.

The bus continued to inch forward and finally made it to the front of the line. As they crossed over, Miguel forced himself to think about what they would do once they reached their stop.

"Natalia," he said, "are you going to call your grandparents when we get to the station?"

Natalia looked over at him and shook her head. "No. They would just send me back." When she didn't offer an alternative, Miguel tried again. "Is there anyone in your family you can call?" Natalia shook her head again, but did not speak.

"I think I can call..." he began, before she interrupted.

"Let's just find someone there who can give us a ride."

Miguel wanted to say "Are you crazy?" but held his tongue. "I...I don't think that's a good idea," he offered instead.

"Miguel," she said, her voice low and hurried, "if we tell our family here, they'll send us back so fast, we'll never get a chance to even look for Benjamín. Please," she pleaded.

Miguel rubbed his face with his palms. What had he done, coming here? He could already feel his head starting to hurt. He looked up at Natalia. "What about the doctor?"

Natalia's eyes widened. "Your grandpa's doctor?"

Miguel nodded. "He's always been really good friends with Abuelo, for as long as I can remember. We can ask him to give us a ride. I don't think our families would think of calling him."

Natalia looked uncertain. "I don't know, Miguel. What if *he* calls *them*?"

Miguel frowned. "I don't think he will."

"Why?"

"I just...don't," Miguel answered. He didn't know why, but he was sure he was right.

After a few moments of silence, Natalia nodded slowly. "Okay," she said uncertainly. "Okay. But if he calls, we leave and don't tell him where we're going."

Miguel nodded. "Okay."

As soon as the bus stopped, Miguel and Natalia shouldered their backpacks and walked quickly to the telephone booths. They had to wait behind a few passengers who had rushed to use the phones ahead of them. When Miguel dialed the doctor's number, the ringing seemed to echo endlessly and bounce off the walls of the station.

"He's not answering," he said to Natalia, looking back at the long line forming behind them. The phone continued to ring and ring.

Natalia followed Miguel's gaze to the line of passengers. "Then we start to walk," she said. "Let me just go to the bathroom." She turned and hurried away.

Miguel hung up the phone and picked it up again, ignoring the groans of irritation of some of the passengers waiting in line. As he began to dial, he realized he was calling his grandfather's house. When the phone began to ring, Miguel stood there, listening. His heart ached as he realized that he was hoping his grandfather would answer. He pulled the phone away from his ear, but then he heard a voice.

"Abuelo?" Miguel said, his heart pounding.

There was a moment of silence, and then: "Miguel?"

There was a sharp pain in Miguel's chest as he realized who it was. "Doctor?"

"Miguel, is everything okay?" the doctor asked. Miguel could hear barks in the background. Conde.

He shook his head. "Doctor, I'm here with Natalia. In Mexico."

More silence.

"Doctor?"

"Yes, I'm here, Miguel."

༄

When Miguel told Natalia about the phone call, she looked almost disappointed to hear that the doctor was coming to pick them up. "But, Miguel, what if he called our parents after you hung up with him?"

"I don't think so," Miguel said.

"Why not?" she asked in an urgent voice.

"I don't know," Miguel said, thinking about his conversation with the doctor. He looked over at her. "The way he was acting, maybe. He said, 'I'm so glad you're finally here,' Natalia."

Natalia frowned. "What's that supposed to mean?"

"It was almost," Miguel thought out loud, "almost as if he'd been waiting for us."

Seven

T HE THREE OF THEM sat squished together in the front of the doctor's small truck..

They had been driving almost half an hour, but Miguel still had not found a way to broach the subject of whether or not the doctor would keep their secret. Natalia kept elbowing him in the ribs, not willing to let him forget.

Finally, Miguel cleared his throat. "Doctor," he began.

The doctor looked over at him, waiting.

"Did you…you didn't…I mean…"

Natalia rolled her eyes.

The doctor raised his eyebrows. "No," he said, "I didn't call your parents." A thoughtful expression crossed his face. "But, if they call me, I don't think I can lie." He looked at

Natalia as he said this, and she quickly turned and gazed out the window, pretending to be fascinated by the shrubs and skinny trees they were passing.

Miguel nodded, his body relaxing. He would have a few days in his grandfather's house. He looked around the truck, taking in the missing pieces of carpet, the oil marks, and a few large red stains. Hung over the rearview mirror was a small string of four garlic bulbs. Miguel reached up, but before he could touch the garlic, the doctor's hand shot out and gripped his wrist so strongly Miguel had to pull away.

"Sorry," the doctor said, his voice gruff. "It's just, you know, it keeps bad spirits away."

Miguel rubbed his wrist. "I thought that was just for the doors of houses."

The doctor raised his eyebrows again. When he spoke, his voice was light again. "Garlic can be used for many things, medicinal and non-medicinal. For use against spirits, in any location."

Miguel laughed. "You can't really believe that."

Something passed over the doctor's face, so quickly that Miguel did not have time to figure out what it was.

He pressed on. "You're a doctor. Of medicine. Science. You can't honestly believe all those stories about spirits and evil demons and things like that."

Natalia shifted next to him, and Miguel realized his mistake. It seemed the doctor did, too.

"Your grandfather did," was his reply.

Miguel looked down at the floor. He moved his shoe and lifted it slightly. A small red smear had appeared on the side. Miguel hunched over to examine the spot on the carpet beneath his feet, but just as he did, the truck stopped suddenly.

"Here we are," the doctor said, his voice gruff.

Miguel looked out the window, a burning sensation slowly filling his stomach and traveling up to his chest. The light green house stood timeless, as if nothing had happened. Miguel let himself pretend, for just a few moments, that he was just visiting his grandfather. That he would find him in the garden watering the flowers, in his brown pants and plaid shirt and his socks and soft sandals, with Conde sniffing the flowers and pawing at the bugs.

The tall bushes in the garden swayed slightly and cast long shadows on the dirt road.

The doctor cleared his throat. Miguel grabbed his backpack and jumped out of the truck before turning to thank the doctor for the ride. The doctor reached up, pulled two garlic bulbs from the string hanging from his rearview mirror, and threw them at Miguel.

"Put them in your bags," the doctor said.

Natalia grabbed one and put it carefully in her backpack. Miguel stood there with the other garlic bulb in his hand, fighting off the sudden urge to crush it.

The doctor's eyes grew dark. "Just do it. Please," he said. Miguel looked at him a few moments more before reaching around and putting it in a zippered pocket of his backpack. The doctor reached over and, without saying another word, slammed the passenger door shut and drove away.

Miguel looked up at the sky. The sun would be going down soon, and clouds were gathering. He felt a few drops on his hands. There was a rumble in the distance. Great, just great. Now it was going to rain.

He quickly opened the gate and strode up to the porch.

"He didn't even ask if we had a way to get inside," Natalia said. She frowned. Miguel reached up to one of the plants hanging on the porch and pulled out a silver key. He looked around the corner to the backyard, where Conde was pacing.

"That's odd," Miguel said, more to himself than to Natalia. "Normally he would have come up by now to see who was here."

Natalia was still frowning.

"What?" Miguel asked.

"Don't you think it's weird?" Natalia asked.

"Well, yeah, I mean, what if we were strangers? He's usually really good about guarding the house."

"No," she said, placing her hand on Miguel's arm. "I mean, the doctor. He didn't ask us anything. He didn't even ask us why we were here."

They were silent for a moment.

"I'm sure he knows," Miguel said finally, but an uneasy feeling began to creep up his spine. He walked back to the gate, looking both ways down the street.

"There's no one," he said.

"What?" Natalia asked, joining him at the gate.

"There's no one out. No one driving, no kids outside, no people, no one. I don't even remember passing a car while we were driving over here in the truck."

"It's like a bad omen," Natalia said.

Miguel shook his head. "Maybe it's the weather. It looks like rain soon. There may be a storm blowing in. We should check before…" He trailed off.

"Before we begin looking," Natalia finished.

Miguel nodded.

As he started to turn, he thought he saw someone looking at them from a gray house across the street. He glanced past the gate again, and he was sure. He couldn't make out if it was a man or a woman—he could just see a large, dark figure. A curtain fell over the window and they were gone.

He tried not to think anything of it. It wasn't until they were inside Abuelo's house, searching for a weather report on the television, that Miguel remembered.

The gray house across the street was abandoned.

Eight

AS THE WIND STARTED to blow that night, Miguel and Natalia tried to lure Conde into the house without success.

"Maybe he's hot," Natalia suggested, even though the temperature had dropped at least fifteen degrees since night had fallen. The weather reports were not hopeful. A storm was coming, and it looked like it would last a few days. Miguel flipped from channel to channel, and every report was the same. Radar flashed across the screen, showing almost the whole of Mexico covered in reds and yellows. The news anchors talked about the giant storm blanket over the country, one of them joking, "*Parece el fin del mundo.*"

Miguel and Natalia watched the news anchors laugh at

the comment, and they both knew the other agreed that, yes, it did seem like the end of the world.

As the rumbles grew louder, Natalia broke the silence. "We should just carry him inside."

It was almost ten o'clock, and it felt like the wind was picking up every minute. Although they didn't know it, they shared almost the same thoughts—wondering how bad the weather would be, wondering how they would get any searching done, wondering if they had made a terrible mistake in coming. Natalia knew that she was going to look for Benjamín in the rain, whether Miguel helped her or not. And Miguel knew he could not stop her.

A low rumble came through the window, and it took Miguel and Natalia a moment to realize it was not thunder. Conde was racing back and forth, his loud growls and barks echoing in the night, breaking through the sound of the howling wind.

"Okay," Miguel said. "We'll just carry him in."

They found Conde hunkered in front of the stone wall that separated the backyard from the canal that ran behind it. The hair on his back was straight up, his teeth glistening in the night. There was a rustle, and Conde growled, leaping up, trying to clear the wall. Another rustle. Miguel and Natalia crept over and peeked over the top of the wall. Someone was crouched on the other side. Miguel almost fell back as they jumped up and ran toward the canal.

"Benjamín!" Natalia yelled, scrambling up the wall. Conde growled even louder, trying to climb next to her. Miguel looked around and grabbed a bucket, turning it upside down for Natalia to put her foot on. As she jumped over, Miguel followed, landing on his feet on the other side. His shoes crunched on something. He looked down and realized they were chicken bones.

He didn't stop to wonder how they got there. He tore after Natalia, who had almost caught up to—whom? Even from this distance Miguel could tell that the proportions of the person were all wrong; they were too small to be Benjamín. The wind roared in his ears, and then he heard a thud as Conde landed on the other side of the wall, chasing after them.

The person—whoever it was—jumped into the canal and dove under the water. Natalia almost jumped in after them, but Miguel grabbed her and held her back.

"Miguel, it's Benjamín!" she screamed, struggling to get away.

Conde caught up and almost passed them, and Miguel had to grab on to him too.

"It's not," he murmured, watching as the person, or creature, finally surfaced halfway across the canal and swam away, impossibly fast. "It's not," he repeated. "Look."

As the figure jumped out of the canal and onto the opposite bank, they turned back. The moon broke through the clouds, shining a light directly on them. Conde growled and Natalia gasped as the light glinted off of the creature's sharp teeth—almost as sharp as Conde's.

"What is that?" Miguel whispered, squinting.

The water began to swirl then, and the howling of the wind made it impossible for Miguel to hear what Natalia said in response. Conde stopped growling and lifted his nose to sniff the air. The moon retreated behind the clouds again. Miguel stood and started pulling Natalia and Conde back toward the house. Though it seemed impossible, it grew even darker, and in the darkness, Miguel and Natalia could make out something moving in the swirling water.

A dark shape began to rise up out of the water. Conde started to move forward, but Miguel pulled him back once more.

"Oh my God," Natalia said, her voice just a whisper, her eyes wide with terror.

"We need to get out of here," Miguel said, dragging her and Conde away. "The storm…"

Natalia shook her head and pointed toward the water. "It's her," she said.

Miguel turned back. A woman in a black dress and red cloak was walking across the water toward them. Her dark, wet hair covered her eyes. She stepped onto the ground in front of them. The water stopped swirling, and the wind grew still. As the moon broke through the clouds again, the woman was illuminated, her red cloak glowing so much that they had to turn away for a moment.

When they looked back, she was standing right in front of them.

Miguel's heart felt as though it was trying to burst out through his throat.

Natalia couldn't look away. "It's La Llorona."

Nine

NATALIA'S FIRST THOUGHT WAS that La Llorona didn't look like a demon at all—she was beautiful. When her hair finally fell away from her eyes, Natalia could see they were bright green.

Natalia's second thought was that, regardless of what she looked like, this demon had taken her brother. That thought overpowered her, and she charged at La Llorona. But there was nothing there. She tripped, falling through nothingness, landing face-first in the canal water.

La Llorona turned, and Natalia scrambled to get out of the water before the specter could drown her. "No, get away from me!" she screamed.

La Llorona stepped back, the lace on the bottom of her

dress dragging on the ground.

Natalia's hands shook as she reached into her front pocket and pulled out a plastic bottle. She fumbled, almost dropping the bottle, but she managed to unscrew the lid and hurl the contents of the bottle at La Llorona.

Nothing happened.

Miguel watched incredulously, still holding on to Conde. This had to be a joke. Someone must know they were back; they either had Benjamín, or they were playing a cruel trick on them. Maybe it was the person he had seen in the house across the street earlier.

"It's...it's supposed to work," Natalia said, her voice trembling even more than her hands. "It's holy water."

Before Miguel could react, the woman spoke. Her voice was strong and deep, yet tired. "That only works on demons."

"But...but you..." Natalia began.

"No, I'm not. Please put it away and save what you have left. You might actually need it later."

Natalia picked up a handful of stones and pebbles off the bank and threw them at the woman. "Where is Benjamín? Where is he? You took him!" When the woman didn't react, Natalia looked around frantically, hoping to find a large stick or some other weapon. Why hadn't the holy water worked?

"I've been waiting for you," the woman said. "Benjamín is the boy that was taken. He is your brother."

"You took him! Please, please just give him back. You don't have to kill him. He is not your child!" Natalia was screaming now. Miguel realized that the wind had completely stopped, and there had not been any more rumbles of thunder.

"Please, calm down," the woman said. "I have been waiting for you. I did not take your brother."

"You lie!" Natalia screamed. "That's what you do. You take them. I heard you! I heard your scream that night. You took him. Please, please don't drown him." She fell to her knees, crying now. "Just give him back. You can take me, but please just give him back."

Miguel started toward her, but the woman raised her hand.

"Natalia, I did not take your brother."

At the sound of her name, Natalia stopped crying. An ugly, cold hand gripped her heart.

"That *was* me you heard that night. I saw your brother being taken. That is why I screamed."

"Wh-what?"

"I did not take your brother," the woman repeated. "But I know who did."

Natalia looked up. "Who?" Her voice was barely above a

whisper.

La Llorona looked around, her eyes stopping across the canal where the person or creature had disappeared into the trees. "It's best if we go inside. It is not safe out here." She turned back and looked at Miguel and Natalia, then at Conde. "There are eyes everywhere."

She started to move toward the wall Natalia and Miguel had scaled. Natalia hurriedly stood. "Why should I believe you? You're a demon!"

The woman stopped and turned. "Then why didn't your holy water work on me?"

"Maybe—maybe it was…" Natalia began.

"No. Holy water only works on demons."

"But you…"

"No. I am not a demon."

Miguel finally spoke. "Natalia, this is just an ordinary woman." He leveled his gaze on La Llorona. "So, either you took Benjamín, or you really do know who took him—" He broke off as he realized, with increasing panic, that the woman was slightly transparent. He could see the intricate lace on her dress, but he could also faintly see the river and the trees through her. "This has to be a trick," he said, studying her dress.

The woman smiled slightly. "You must be Miguel."

He stepped back, pulling Conde with him. "Who are

you?" he asked.

"Your friend Natalia already identified me."

Miguel shook his head. "La Llorona is not real."

She looked straight at him. "Is that what your grandfather told you?"

Miguel was quiet.

"That's what I thought. Despite what you've heard," she looked at Miguel, then at Natalia, "I am not a demon. There are truths, as well as fabrications, in every legend. My story is no exception." The woman stopped and looked up at the sky. "It's getting late, and the more time we spend out here, the harder it will be to find Benjamín." She looked up at the tops of the trees, which had begun to sway as the wind picked up again.

"Natalia, please, I know it's hard to believe, after what you've been told your whole life. But understand, truths tend to become bent over the years. Yes, I was a woman long ago, but I am not a demon now. There is something at work here—something much more terrible than what you believe me to be. And it has taken your brother. Please, let me help you get him back."

Natalia was quiet for a moment. Thunder rumbled in the distance once again. Finally, Natalia nodded and started to follow La Llorona toward the house.

"Wait," Miguel said, not moving. "There is no way you

are going into my grandfather's house without telling us who you are, and what you saw out here."

The woman stopped. She turned and looked at Miguel. "My name was Maria, once."

"Oh, please," Miguel said.

The woman moved so quickly that Miguel fell back on the dirt. Her face was an inch from his, and he could see the moon and the clouds through her head.

"My condolences for the loss of your grandfather," she whispered. "If he were here, we wouldn't be wasting so much time. He would have already let me in his house." She moved gracefully back. Miguel's hand shot out, and he tried to grab her arm, but his hand passed through her.

"Who are you?" he asked again.

She turned away. "La Llorona," she said finally, her voice tired and sad.

Ten

WHEN THEY HAD ALMOST reached the house, Natalia pulled Miguel aside. "It's okay," she said breathlessly. "Remember, your grandpa has all those garlic strings and things over the door. If she's a demon, she won't be able to come inside. I can get holy water from the jar in his room and—"

Miguel cut her off. "She's not La Llorona, Natalia," he whispered. "She's not a demon, either. She's just some crazy woman. But maybe she saw something and wants money or food. Maybe she can really help us."

Despite what he'd seen on the side of the canal, Miguel was convinced that this woman was only pretending to be the Weeping Woman. It had to be some kind of trick. His mind kept thinking of reasons why she would try to fool them like this—maybe she knew something, or she had Benjamín, or someone put her up to it. Even if she really believed she was La Llorona, how would she know that Natalia's brother had gone missing? She had to be up to something.

The phone was ringing as they stepped through the door. Miguel rushed to answer it, but the woman suddenly appeared in front of it.

"It's the doctor," she said. "Don't tell him I'm here."

She moved aside and Miguel put the phone to his ear. "Hello?"

"Miguel, it's me," said the doctor. "I just wanted to check on you. The weather is a little rough right now. You and Natalia aren't planning on going anywhere soon, are you?"

The woman stood in front of Miguel, shaking her head no.

"No," Miguel said.

The doctor was silent.

"Is someone there with you?"

Miguel frowned. Why would he ask that? Thoughts began to fill his head. What if this woman and the doctor were working together? What if they had taken Benjamín? His eyes fell on a picture of his grandfather with the doctor from when they were in their twenties. He remembered his grandfather telling him that the doctor had given a group of kids all the money he had in his wallet when they had come across them trying to steal the radio from Abuelo's old truck. No, the doctor couldn't have taken Benjamín. Could he?

"No," Miguel answered.

The doctor was silent again.

"I'll be by to check on you in the morning." Click. The line went dead.

The woman's eyebrows were raised. "He will probably be coming by sometime in the middle of the night. We must leave before then."

"The doctor?" Natalia asked. "But why? And why should we leave before then?"

The woman was looking at Miguel, and he felt as though she was reading his doubts about the doctor.

"The doctor was a good friend to your grandfather," she said slowly.

Miguel nodded. He felt uneasy. The doctor had sounded strange. Something about his words had brought Miguel back to reality. What was he thinking, letting a strange woman into the house?

"Miguel," the woman said. "I know it is hard for you to believe, but I am not human. And the doctor, he is a good man, but…"

"But what?" Natalia asked.

"But, like me, he knows more about this."

Miguel sat down, patting the couch so that Conde could jump up next to him. He stroked his fur, finding comfort in his presence. He knew that if Conde had reacted differently to this woman—if he had growled even once—he would not have let her in the house. Instead, when the woman approached the couch and sat down, Conde wagged his tail. Did he know this woman?

Natalia sat down slowly and waited. Even inside the house, the woman was transparent.

"We don't have a lot of time," the woman began, then paused. She closed her eyes, then sighed. "How much do you know…" She hesitated.

"What?" Natalia asked, impatient.

"How much do you know about the tlahuelpocmimi?"

"The vampires?" Natalia asked.

Miguel sat upright. The tlahuelpuchi?

"That's right," the woman said, turning to look at Miguel. "The vampires."

Natalia looked at Miguel. "You've heard of them, right?"

Miguel almost laughed. Of course he'd heard of them. That was probably Abuelo's favorite legend to tell around the fire. He'd heard about those vampires a million times.

Miguel nodded.

"Of course you've heard of them," the woman said, echoing Miguel's thoughts. "Your grandfather would have known a lot about them."

Natalia spoke. "They're vampires, but a little different from ones like Dracula. They aren't bitten—they're just born as vampires. And they have to drink blood to survive. Usually from babies." Natalia made a face.

"What do you know about them, Miguel?" the woman asked, facing him.

Miguel took a deep breath. He couldn't believe he was having this conversation. "They're usually women," he finally added.

"Very good," the woman said. "I'm sure your grandfather would be proud you were paying attention."

Miguel blinked.

The woman turned her body to face Natalia, and the words she spoke next came quickly and urgently. "Natalia, that is what has taken your brother."

Natalia shook her head. "But... I thought... I mean, Benjamín is not a baby."

The woman shook her head. "The ones that are taken do not have to be babies. They can take children, even older children."

Miguel rubbed his eyes to keep from rolling them.

"Miguel?" the woman addressed him. "Do you have something to say?"

Miguel placed his hand over his mouth, the words "You've got to be kidding me" almost escaping from it.

"I just," he finally said, "I just don't think…"

"That any of this is real," the woman finished for him.

Natalia looked at Miguel, her eyes desperate and sad.

"Natalia, I…"

"Please, Miguel. Please."

Miguel looked down at the floor, not wanting to hear the pleading in her voice. The same pleading tone he'd heard in his own mind as he asked for his grandfather to come back.

"What else do we have to go on?" Natalia asked.

Miguel nodded. "Okay," he said to the woman. "But how do you know a tlahuelpuchi took Benjamín?"

The woman's voice was weary as she answered. "Because that's what took my children."

Eleven

"SO LET ME GET this straight," Miguel said, trying to keep the skepticism from his voice and hoping he sounded somewhat supportive. "This tlahuelpuchi needs to eat once a month and takes children. That is what took Benjamín, and also what took your own children so long ago?"

La Llorona nodded. Raising her hand, she added, "Not the same one, of course. There are many alive at one time, and they do eventually die."

"Right," Miguel said, making an effort to believe that what was happening was real. "But, if you don't mind me asking, if you didn't drown your children, then why are you still here? On earth?"

"Eventually I did die," La Llorona replied. "I just...never left. I never found my children. I still look for them now." She turned to Natalia. "I must admit, that is part of why I am here. For years, after I realized what was taking children, what took my own children, I tried to find out where the tlahuelpocmimi live. Other than the fact that many of them live in or near the state of Tlaxcala, I have been lost. I realized some time ago that I needed to find out where children were disappearing from, who took them, and where. I should have followed that chaneque you saw. He might have been working for a tlahuelpuchi."

Miguel shook his head. "The person we saw crossing the canal?"

Natalia broke in, "But I thought chaneques and duendes were good. Troublemakers maybe, but...not evil."

"Some of them turn bad," La Llorona replied, and silence fell over the room. Conde had jumped to the floor and stretched out, flopping on his side, almost asleep. Miguel looked at the clock above the television. It was almost midnight.

"So, if the vampires live in Tlaxcala, we just need to go there," Natalia said slowly.

Miguel almost laughed. "Natalia, it's not that simple. That's still a big place, especially if you don't know what you're looking for."

La Llorona motioned to the clock. "We need to leave soon."

"You just said you don't know where exactly these vampires live," Miguel said, a little too loudly.

"Not to Tlaxcala. We need to find someone who can help us. Someone who will know where these vampires may be. I've been thinking for some time that since there is always violence and suffering around these vampires, someone who is familiar with that might know where to find them."

"Who?" Natalia asked, sitting on the edge of the couch. Her hands were gripping her knees so tightly that her knuckles were white.

"Death."

Miguel looked up at that. As if she knew what he was thinking, La Llorona turned to him. "Death might be the one person who could tell us where to find the tlahuelpocmimi."

"And...and you know where Death is?" Miguel asked carefully. If this was really happening—if this was all real, if Death could be found somewhere—then he would know where Abuelo was. Maybe he could even bring him back.

La Llorona looked at Miguel, and for a moment, he thought he saw pity in her eyes. "I don't," she finally said. "But I know someone who does. I've been avoiding him.

We haven't spoken in centuries. But if anyone knows Death, it's him."

"Who?" Natalia asked, her eyes wide.

"My husband," La Llorona said, her face almost blank. "El Charro."

Miguel was pulled out of his thoughts. "El Charro?!" he practically yelled.

"The demon?" Natalia asked.

La Llorona nodded. "The demon."

The clock began to strike midnight, and La Llorona stood. Conde sat up, almost as if he had been waiting for her. "Bring your backpacks," she instructed Miguel and Natalia. "I've heard rumors, and if they're correct, El Charro will be appearing right about now. I can take us there, quickly."

Miguel and Natalia stood and grabbed their backpacks. La Llorona spread her cloak out around them, the soft red cloth covering them completely like large wings. Fear began to grip Miguel. What if this woman was La Llorona? Or worse, what if she was some demon whose hands they had just willingly walked into? But as Conde joined them under the cloak and Miguel held onto him, he hoped that maybe this woman—La Llorona—might really be able to take them to Death, and to Abuelo.

El Charro
THE HORSEMAN

EVERYONE SAID MARIBEL WAS the most beautiful girl in the village. Maribel was so kind, so sweet, so generous, so much fun. Only her parents knew, however, that though Maribel was beautiful, she had a dark side. They would plead with her not to stay out too late, and not to go too far with strangers. Maribel was quick to anger, and she did not like anyone telling her what to do or who she should and should not talk to. After all, someone as beautiful as she should be allowed to do whatever she wanted.

Maribel loved to be admired, and she had many admirers. She knew that one day she would meet a handsome man who would buy her whatever she wanted and take her away from the small village where she had lived all her life. One night Maribel went out in her nicest red dress, which made her black hair and eyes shine, enhancing her beauty. As she danced, she noticed a handsome man standing against the wall, watching her. He was tall, with dark hair and eyes, and was wearing a black charro suit lined with silver threads. A small patch of red on his white shirt seemed to glow in the night. Maribel knew instantly that she was in love. She knew this was the man she would spend the rest of her life with.

As Maribel's friends began to go home, they asked her if she wanted to walk home with them. But the man approached her, and Maribel waved her friends away, winking and assuring them she would have someone to walk her home.

The man bowed and kissed Maribel's hand. "Forgive me, but I could not take my eyes off of you," he said to her in a low voice. Maribel tried to hide her smile. "It would be an honor to walk you home," he said. Maribel nodded. Outside, the man untied his horse, a tall black stallion with a black-and-silver saddle. The man invited Maribel up to ride, but she shook her head. She didn't want to risk getting her beautiful red dress dirty. The man's eyes flashed, but it happened so quickly Maribel thought she had imagined it.

As they walked through the deserted streets, the man asked Maribel many questions about herself. Did she have any brothers or sisters, where did she work, what did she do for enjoyment, what were her dreams, how did she become so beautiful? Maribel's cheeks flushed as he flattered her, and as they walked they drew nearer and nearer to each other. A jingling sound came from a bag attached to the horse's saddle, and when Maribel asked what was making the noise, the man leaned close to her, as if telling her a secret.

"Coins. Tomorrow I will buy a nearby ranch, and a few other things."

Maribel's eyes glistened. This was the man for her. As they stopped in front of her house, Maribel saw that the curtain was pulled back and her parents were looking out the window, waiting for her. She rolled her eyes in irritation as the curtain fell back. She knew her parents were coming down to open the door, to ask her what she was doing walking so late at night with a strange man.

"Will you come with me?" the man asked her, almost breathlessly. He looked up at the window where her parents had been standing.

Before she could stop herself, Maribel replied, "Yes!"

The man helped her up on the horse and then climbed up

in front of her. As they began to gallop away, the front door opened and her parents ran after her. "Maribel, no! That man is El Charro!"

Maribel laughed. "Can you believe them? They still believe in those legends."

The man laughed, but as Maribel put her arms around him, she felt a hole in his chest where the red patch had been. She looked at his face, and in the moonlight she saw his skull through his transparent skin. He turned to look at her, still laughing. Maribel tried to free herself and jump off the horse, but she couldn't. She could see her parents fading away in the background. Maribel felt her heart pulsing as she remembered what her parents had always told her about El Charro. *El Charro is a demon that takes the hearts of women that fall in love with him and devours them, filling the void left by his own lack of a heart.*

Twelve

THERE WAS A STRONG rush of wind, and Natalia's stomach lurched. She covered her mouth as they seemed to dip down and fall to the ground. Miguel put both of his arms around Conde, trying to ignore the ache in his feet. Without warning the wind stopped and they fell to the ground, rolling and kicking up dirt and rocks. Conde was the first to jump up and shake himself off. As Miguel and Natalia stood and dusted the dirt off of their pants, a low growl escaped Conde's throat.

They were surrounded by trees that seemed to go on endlessly. It took a moment for their eyes to adjust, and Miguel was still blinking when Natalia asked, "Where are we?"

"Guanajuato," La Llorona replied. Miguel noticed her feet were not touching the ground; she was floating slightly above it.

Conde growled again. Miguel thought he heard leaves crunching, but he couldn't be sure.

"El Charro is here, in this forest?" Natalia asked.

La Llorona nodded slightly. She seemed to be straining to hear as well. She lowered herself to the ground and began to walk. "This way," she said, and Conde began to follow her. Miguel looked around, his eyes still having trouble adjusting to this much darkness.

"The last I heard, he was here, undoubtedly trying to find more hearts to keep himself alive," La Llorona said bitterly.

"But…" Natalia began, then seemed to think better of it.

"But why is he my husband?" La Llorona finished Natalia's train of thought.

Natalia nodded.

There was silence.

"Is he like you?" Miguel asked. "Has his story been changed as it's been retold over time?"

La Llorona sighed. "What have you heard of him?"

"That he's a demon," Miguel said.

"And that he…he eats the hearts of women," Natalia added.

"Better watch out, Natalia," Miguel said, chuckling.

"Miguel!" Natalia hissed.

"No, Natalia," La Llorona said, her voice heavy with something that made Miguel stop laughing. "Miguel's right. You should heed his warning."

"But then…" Natalia began again.

"He was the one I fell in love with. I thought he had changed. I thought he had become a good man. We had three children together. They were taken one night, while he was out. Taken by a tlahuelpuchi." Her voice had an edge to it that kept Miguel and Natalia from asking any more. "I never found out what he was doing that night, where he was. I went after my children, with nothing but the clothes on my back, and I never saw him again. If he had been home—if he had been there—he could have saved them."

Through the darkness there was a small *crack*, as if someone had stepped on a stick and broken it in half.

La Llorona stopped, and Conde let out a soft growl. She placed her hand on Conde's head and he grew still. Natalia and Miguel strained to see what was there in the darkness, but they couldn't make anything out.

"You might as well show yourself," La Llorona said loudly. "The dog knows you're here."

There was silence. Then there came a sort of clinking sound, like spurs on cowboy boots. It echoed around them, though neither Miguel nor Natalia could figure out where it was coming from. As Conde and La Llorona turned around to face Miguel, he realized that it had stopped directly behind him.

La Llorona placed her hand gently on Conde's head, calming him. Natalia's eyes widened and her mouth opened slightly, making Miguel hesitate before he turned around. When he finally did, he had to back away in order to look up at the man standing there. Miguel's eyes went from the shiny black boots with silver spurs to the black-and-silver charro suit, to the white shirt, to the shadowed face with dark hair and red eyes, and finally to the black-and-silver sombrero. The man had to be at least six feet tall, and behind him loomed a large black horse.

Everyone stood in silence for a few moments. The man looked at them one by one, his eyes finally resting on La Llorona.

"Maria," he said, his voice gruff from disuse, "it's been a long time."

La Llorona's voice wavered when she spoke. "I need to find Death."

The man raised his eyebrows. "Had enough of this world?" he said with a laugh.

"It's not for me," La Llorona snapped back. "Another child has been taken."

The man stood up straighter at this. "Where?"

"In Valle Hermoso. It was Natalia's young brother, Benjamín." She gestured toward Natalia. "It was very strange. He is not a baby."

The man's eyes widened and he stepped closer to the group.

There was another small *crack,* and the man motioned for them to be quiet.

When everything was still again, he continued. "A child was taken near here not too long ago, also not a baby." He hesitated, then moved closer still. "Something is happening. Not just in these woods, but all over the country. The creatures...some of them are behaving... strangely. And the vampires, they are crossing more and more boundaries. It's almost as if..."

"What? What is it?" La Llorona asked, a slight note of panic in her voice.

The man looked at Miguel and then at Natalia.

"It's all right," La Llorona said. "This boy, Miguel. His grandfather was Abraham."

The man raised his eyebrows. "*Was?*"

La Llorona nodded.

The man looked at Miguel again, then off into the darkness. "It's almost as if something is happening," he said. "Something bringing them out."

A look of fear flickered on La Llorona's face, but she said calmly, "I think if we can find Death, he might be able to tell us where the tlahuelpocmimi are. At least the one that took Natalia's brother."

The man nodded. "And that's why you came to find me." He laughed bitterly. "Of course this demon could help you find Death. Is that what you thought?"

"I'm right, aren't I?" La Llorona asked, her voice cold, one eyebrow raised.

The man's smile faded. "I know where Death is. But what makes you think I would help you? After all this time, why should I?"

"You owe me this," La Llorona said.

"I don't owe you anything," the man replied quickly. "You left the night our children disappeared. I never heard from you again. What do I owe you?"

"You were gone that night, who knows where!" La Llorona shouted.

The man flinched, looking around. "Quiet!" he hissed. "All right, just be quiet."

Another *crack*, then silence again.

La Llorona narrowed her eyes suspiciously. "What are you doing out here?"

The man raised one hand in the air for them to keep quiet. Another *crack*. Silence.

"I had heard rumors that you were hunting things out in these forests. Is that true?"

"I'm following a chaneque," he replied in a low voice. "They're usually kind, unless their property is trespassed upon. But lately...lately more of them have been...going rogue."

Miguel looked over at Natalia, and he could tell she was also thinking about the creature they saw by the canal.

"Look, just tell us where Death is, and I'll take them there," La Llorona said. She sounded like a tired mother.

"Oh, yes, because you can just walk up to Death and start a conversation."

"And why not?" La Llorona demanded. "I *am* supernatural."

"Oh, I don't know," the man said in a mocking tone. "Maybe because of a little thing called a soul."

"What?"

"A soul. You still have one, don't you?"

"And what does that have to do with anything?"

The man gestured toward Miguel and Natalia. "It's safer if someone without a soul approaches Death first."

"What are you trying to say?" La Llorona asked.

The man sighed. "I'm saying, my dear Maria, that I need to come with you."

Thirteen

"I'M NOT LEAVING MY horse," El Charro said for the third time.

"Of course. You wouldn't dare leave without your horse," La Llorona muttered.

"*Ya vas a empezar?*" El Charro asked. "If you're going to start, I can just stay here. I was close to catching up with someone I've been watching for a long time, and you made me fall behind."

La Llorona rolled her eyes. "Fine. Fine. The sooner we find Death, the better."

"If you say so," retorted El Charro.

Miguel and Natalia kept exchanging glances. Conde walked alongside La Llorona, and every so often he released a low growl in the direction of El Charro.

"Is he in this forest?" La Llorona asked.

El Charro shook his head. "No. At this time of night, he's probably in the capital."

"Then let's get going," La Llorona said, and a breeze started to pick up.

Natalia felt a heavy weight settle in her stomach. El Charro raised one hand. "That draws too much attention." He motioned at the leaves beginning to lift off the ground. "We need to travel quietly."

Miguel couldn't help but feel grateful. He didn't think he could stand another trip by flight, especially *that* kind of flight.

He fell into step beside Natalia. She whistled low, and Conde slowed, trotting between them. As they walked, Natalia opened her backpack and pulled out the picture of Benjamín, stroking it softly with her fingers. Miguel pretended to be interested in the leaves on the trees as they walked, but Conde moved closer to Natalia and nuzzled her left arm with his snout. She returned the picture to her backpack pocket and zipped it closed, turning toward the darkness to wipe the tears from her eyes. Miguel fought the urge to place his arm on her shoulder, not wanting to interrupt her private moment. Instead, he looked back to his other companions. La Llorona and El Charro were both glancing back at him, their eyebrows raised. He flushed with embarrassment.

It still seemed unreal. Everything *felt* real enough; the leaves of the forest were solid beneath his hand, and he could still feel the nausea in his stomach from the flight to the forest. But how was it possible that they could be here in such a short amount of time? How was it possible that La Llorona was here with them? Miguel pinched himself and, although it hurt, he still couldn't quite trust that this was actually happening. In his mind, he was asleep at his grandfather's house, summer vacation was not over yet, and he was going to wake up any moment and find that Abuelo was okay and that it was almost time to go back to school. Admitting that this was reality was almost too horrible to think about. Because if it was, it meant that not only was his grandfather gone, but Benjamín was in the hands of a vampire that drank the blood of children. And if the tlahuelpuchi was exactly like the legend he heard growing up, then it drank the blood of children on or near the full moon, which had already passed. Did that mean that Benjamín…?

No. He couldn't think of that.

"Miguel." Natalia's soft voice broke into his thoughts. She pointed up at the sky. "The moon. It's…it's not really full anymore."

Miguel swallowed. So she was thinking the same thing.

El Charro and La Llorona had been quiet as they walked, but now El Charro turned around. "It's not uncommon for the vampires to hold the children for some time. They don't...they don't necessarily...*feed* right away." He patted his horse.

Natalia nodded, and Miguel could almost see the relief on her face. *I hope he's right*, Miguel thought, trying to block out the image of Benjamín in some cold, concrete room, waiting for a vampire to come for him.

A few moments later, Natalia gestured toward La Llorona and El Charro, who'd gone back to exchanging barbs with one another in low voices. "I can see them being a couple," she whispered. "They look pretty striking together."

For the first time, Miguel took a really good look at them. El Charro was at least six and a half feet tall, and his clothes were a deep, clean black. The silver trim shone in the moonlight, and small specks of red could be seen on random parts of his suit. His black hat, also decorated with silver, somehow seemed even darker than his suit. The black lace dress La Llorona wore was the same shade as her dark hair. Her skin shimmered, and Miguel wondered if it had always done so, or if it was a result of her being a spirit. He could see them motioning animatedly with their hands, and for a moment he was back home with his parents. They were arguing now, and Miguel wished he could turn around and run away. Their voices rose in the darkness.

"I was out looking for…something. I can't—I just can't say."

"Oh, but it was so important that you left your family, and our children were taken. Probably taken because you were not there."

"Don't you think I know that? What do you think I have been doing all this time?"

"Stealing the hearts of women, I'm sure," La Llorona shouted in the darkness.

"No. No. You just… you don't understand."

"And I never will, because you will never tell me!"

"I can't. I just can't! Death, he…there's something wrong…"

"Death? What does Death have to do with this?"

There was a loud *crack*.

El Charro turned, his horse's eyes flashing a bright red. "What is it?" he asked. The horse stamped his front hoof on the ground. El Charro looked into the darkness ahead.

"Someone knows we're here," he whispered.

"Someone?" La Llorona echoed. "Who?"

In the blink of an eye, El Charro whipped off his sombrero and laid it on the ground. His horse placed a hoof on the brim of the hat.

"Everyone put your hands on the sombrero," El Charro instructed. "Now!"

Miguel and Natalia began to reach down, but Miguel stopped. There was something coming toward them. A figure in white. As it drew closer, Miguel felt himself pulled toward it. "It can't be," he murmured. "Is it…?"

"Miguel!" Natalia screamed, reaching up and dragging his hand down. Miguel barely had enough time to grab Conde's paw to place on the hat.

"Death!" El Charro said loudly into the night, his voice commanding.

Natalia had just touched the brim when the leaves under her feet changed to gray stone. The horse's hooves clopped on the stone, and Conde began to growl. The moon was more visible than it had been in the forest, and as Natalia looked around she found that they were surrounded by tall buildings, deep orange in color.

"Here?" La Llorona asked.

Natalia's eyes widened as they turned to face the small alley which ended in a narrow set of stairs. "I know this place," she said, her voice full of wonder. "My grandparents brought us here once. They'd been here before they were married, and they wanted us to see it."

Miguel looked around. He had never seen this place

before in his life.

"El Callejón del Beso," Natalia said in awe.

Miguel looked toward the stairs. It couldn't be. Were they really in the city now?

He felt his breath catch in his throat as he looked up toward the legendary set of stairs, where countless people had promised each other eternal love. On the third step, in the middle of the cool night, stood a large, looming black shadow. Slowly, very slowly, the shadow began to turn toward them, its right hand revealing a tall wooden stick with a metal blade on the end—a scythe.

As the figure began to take shape before their eyes, the world grew quiet and still. Miguel knew who this was, beyond a shadow of a doubt.

This was Death.

fourteen

N O ONE SAID A WORD. It was as if none of them dared move, none of them dared breathe. Natalia felt as if they had come at a bad time, almost as if they had interrupted some sacred, special moment. The figure remained silent, his cloak moving slightly in the soft wind.

Conde moved forward before Miguel could stop him, trotting forward until he reached the first step. The figure looked down at the dog as he sniffed the scythe. Miguel moved forward, his hand outstretched. "No, don't…" he began.

El Charro grabbed Miguel by the arm. "It's not the scythe, Miguel." When Miguel didn't understand, El Charro explained, "It's not the scythe that takes them. It's…it's his hands."

As Miguel watched, Conde finished sniffing and turned back to the group. Death still had not spoken.

Miguel blinked in the silence. The moon hid behind clouds and then came back out, the shape almost blurring into the darkness.

"Death," El Charro finally said, his voice cautious. "I—we came for your help."

Death still did not move. La Llorona spoke up. "More children have gone missing, and we know the tlahuelpocmimi are responsible. This girl—Natalia—her brother was taken just recently. Benjamín is his name. Do you know...have you..." She trailed off.

Natalia stepped forward, her voice so loud and strong Miguel stepped back. "Death, sir, please, my brother was taken, and I know...you would know if he...if he had passed on. Sir, please, do you know Benjamín? Here, I have a picture." She unzipped her backpack pocket and took out the picture. With quick steps she walked forward and handed it to the black shape. When he did not take it, she held it up, her thin arm reaching as high as it could in order to hold the picture in front of the cloaked figure. "Do you know him?" she repeated.

Miguel held his breath. Death could reach out and touch her and she would be gone. The shadow had not made a sound since they arrived. How did they know they wouldn't all die right here and now? How did they know that they could trust this specter?

"Natalia," Miguel started to say, but then the figure moved. It happened so quickly Miguel would have missed it if he had blinked. The picture was gone from Natalia's hands, and the cloaked hands of the figure were holding it up to his dark, hooded face.

"Benjamín," came his voice. It was such a heavy voice. Miguel felt its weight in the air. The figure shook his head slowly. "I do not know him," he finally said. He handed the picture back to Natalia, who smiled, tears running down her face. "Yet," the figure added.

Natalia's eyes widened.

"Death, we need to find the vampire that took Benjamín, and we thought maybe you knew where to find them in Tlaxcala? Maybe, even, how to destroy them?" La Llorona said.

Death moved his head, and Miguel felt his eyes looking at him.

El Charro followed Death's gaze.

After some hesitation, he cleared his throat and said, "That is Miguel. Abraham's grandson."

"Abraham?" Death's voice was low.

El Charro nodded.

Miguel's heart raced. This was his chance. "You...you know my grandfather?"

Death stayed silent for so long Miguel wanted to scream. Finally, there came a nod.

"I know Abraham," he replied in his deep, gravelly voice. The voice rumbled through him, and something inside of Miguel broke. If this was true, all of it, then his grandfather was really dead. His grandfather had walked the last walk with Death, and he was gone.

As if he was a spectator standing behind the group, he saw himself choke, saw the tears roll down his cheeks. He saw himself fall to the ground, saw Natalia's eyes widen and El Charro and La Llorona step away. "Please," he heard himself cough. "Please, can he just come back, can you bring him back?"

Death did not move. "I cannot."

"Then—then can I—can you take me to him? Please," Miguel begged. "Please."

Death looked down at him, then at El Charro. "It is not your time."

Natalia placed her hands around Miguel and Conde licked his tears. "Please," Miguel said again.

The echoes of Miguel's coughs and gasps were the only sounds for what seemed like forever, bouncing off the walls of the small alley. Death turned to look up the stairs, at the balconies that almost touched, then turned back, stepping down to the second, then the first step. As the shadow loomed in front of them, Natalia realized that, unlike El Charro and La Llorona, Death was not transparent. His cloak was as dark as the forest they had just come from.

"I can help you find the boy," Death finally said into the darkness.

El Callejón del Beso

THE ALLEY OF THE KISS

IGNACIO WAS THE HARDEST working young man in the city. Although he did not have much, he woke up early every morning and came back late into the night to help his mother and father, who were growing too old to be able to work with their hands for much longer. One day, when he stopped to buy fruit for lunch at a market, he spotted the most beautiful woman he had ever seen in his life. She wore a green lace dress which made her face glow. Her black shiny hair was decorated with a bright red flower. As she walked away, Ignacio decided he must know her name.

He began to follow her, as quickly as he could, but he soon

lost her in the large crowd. Not knowing which way she had gone, Ignacio decided to return to the market to ask if anyone knew her name.

"You must be referring to Catalina," an old woman said, smiling knowingly. "Yes, you can find her around here a few times a week, buying things for her mother and father."

Ignacio could not believe his luck.

"Do you know when she will return?" he asked her.

"No, I'm so sorry," the woman said. As Ignacio's face fell, she added, "She does not live too far from here—about three streets to the east, in a bright orange building. You cannot miss it."

As Ignacio turned to leave, the woman grabbed his arm and pulled him back with a strength Ignacio would not have thought possible.

"You must be careful," the woman said, lowering her voice. "Catalina's father, he wants nothing but the best for her. He can be..." she paused. "Unreasonable."

Ignacio nodded and thanked the woman. He turned to leave, then stopped, wondering if it would be a good idea if he took Catalina some flowers when he went to introduce himself. He turned to ask the woman, but she was gone.

❧

Ignacio tried to stand tall as he raised his hand to knock on the door. His left hand held the flowers he had brought for Catalina—all red. When she opened the door, the flowers fell to the ground as Ignacio gasped. She smiled as she bent down to pick them up, and Ignacio rushed to gather them. "Please forgive me," he said, his voice fast and trembling. His heart had never felt anything like this before.

"Are you looking for someone?" Catalina asked, her voice smooth.

Ignacio nodded. "Yes. You—you don't know me, my name is Ignacio, but I saw you at the market and..." He stopped. What was he going to say? Suddenly he felt that anything he would say might make him sound like a stranger that was following her around the city—but in a way, wasn't he? Ignacio felt his cheeks grow hot and he looked down at the tattered flowers in his hand.

"These are for you," he said in a defeated voice.

Catalina smiled, extending her hand. "They're beautiful," she said, bringing them up to her face and inhaling slowly. "My favorite."

Ignacio nodded and said, "*Buenas noches,*" before turning

and walking away down the steps. What was he thinking? There was nothing he could say that would make him seem like anything other than a crazy stranger who had followed Catalina around.

Days passed, and Ignacio still woke early to go to work, coming back late every night. But Ignacio knew that something had changed. Something was different. There was a sadness that followed him throughout the day, and he found himself wondering what Catalina was doing, what kinds of things she enjoyed and how she spent her free time.

Weeks had gone by before Ignacio finally visited the market again. Gathering mangoes in a bag, he felt a tap on his shoulder and turned. The mangoes dropped to the ground as he saw Catalina standing in front of him, a red flower in her hair. He bent down quickly to gather them up as Catalina did the same, and their heads bumped together.

"Forgive me," Ignacio said, not daring to look her in the eye.

As they stood and Ignacio closed the bag of mangoes, Catalina motioned to the red flower in her hair.

"The flowers you brought me stayed alive much longer than the ones I pick," she said. "I've been hoping to run into you to see if you might be able to show me the spot where you picked them."

Ignacio knew this couldn't be real. This was not happening.

"So?" she asked, motioning for them to begin walking.

Ignacio nodded, paid for the mangoes, and fell into step beside her.

"It's such a beautiful day," Catalina said, looking up at the bright blue sky. "I love the sun, don't you? I love the warmth." Ignacio nodded. Catalina laughed and nodded, teasing him.

Ignacio turned and they followed a trail to a small park. There was a tiny stone bridge over the water, and as they reached the other side, the trail led to the left.

"Is this still part of the park?" Catalina asked, looking around at the tall trees.

"No, not really," Ignacio said. "But this is where the best flowers grow."

Catalina gasped when the flowers came into view. Hundreds of them, all different colors. She ran to the red flowers and bent down, inhaling deeply.

"This is incredible," she said, turning to Ignacio, who had stopped and was watching her.

"Here," she said, handing him a flower. As he came closer to sniff the flower, Catalina tucked it behind his ear, smiling at him.

From that day on, Catalina and Ignacio spent every free moment together. Ignacio woke up extra early just so he would be able to spend more time with her.

Sometimes they would walk to the park and beyond; sometimes they would buy fruit at the market; sometimes their footsteps could be heard long into the night as they walked through the city, talking about where they might live when they were married.

Every night Ignacio waited at the bottom of the steps as Catalina walked up to her door. Always, on the third step, she would turn and pull the flower out of her hair, tossing it to him.

One night, as Catalina turned to toss her flower, the door to her house opened. Her father's tall figure blocked the light inside the house, casting a long shadow over Catalina and Ignacio. He stormed down the stairs, his boots thudding heavily, and brushed past Catalina, who reached for his arm.

"*Papá, por favor,*" Catalina said in a pleading voice.

"Catalina, this has gone on long enough." He turned to look at Ignacio. "Boy, I know you like my daughter, but you need to forget about her. Catalina is going to marry another man."

"Papá—"

"At the end of this month," Catalina's father finished.

"But, sir, I love—"

"You'll love many women in this life, son. Forget about this one." Catalina's father turned and started up the steps. Ignacio reached up and grabbed his arm.

"Don't touch me," the man said, his voice filled with such hatred that Ignacio pulled away. "It's enough that I let such filth near my daughter. Don't touch me again, boy, do you understand?" He looked up at Catalina, then turned back to face Ignacio. "You can't possibly believe that, with your background, with the parents you have, you could possibly give Catalina everything she deserves?"

Ignacio was silent.

"Her husband will. Now get out of here, boy. Catalina, inside."

Ignacio watched as Catalina's father dragged her up the stairs, the flower falling from her hair, the petals covering the steps.

As the light turned on in a room upstairs, Catalina ran out onto her balcony.

"Ignacio!" she called in a whisper.

Ignacio crept closer to hear her.

"Meet me here tomorrow, when the moon is out." She turned and ran back inside, closing the door to the balcony behind her.

❧

Ignacio's mother placed her hands on his shoulders, trying to convince him to wait a few days. "Catalina's father will calm down, you will see," she said hopefully. But Ignacio's father said nothing. He had lived long enough to know that there was nothing that would keep Ignacio from going to see Catalina that night.

Ignacio walked under the full moon, past the park and into the small garden where he picked Catalina's flowers. He took a handful of them this night, hoping that maybe his mother was right. Maybe Catalina's father would be in a better mood tonight.

Ignacio walked down the narrow alley and started to climb the steps. He was on the third step when he heard Catalina's voice above him on the balcony.

"Ignacio," she said softly. She started to climb over the balcony.

"Catalina, no!" Ignacio said in a loud whisper. "What are

you doing?"

"Shhh," she said, putting her finger to her lips. "I'm just going to cross over to the other balcony."

"But your father—" Ignacio began.

"Ignacio, please, just listen. My father is never going to change his mind. If we are going to be together, if we have any chance of being happy, we must leave tonight. Please. I'll just cross over, and then go down the stairs to you."

Ignacio saw the sadness and the fear in her eyes.

"Catalina, you don't—"

"Ignacio, I am only afraid that we will get caught."

Ignacio was silent.

"Now please promise," she said, "if I fall you will catch me."

Ignacio nodded. "I promise."

As Catalina put one foot forward to balance herself on the balcony across from hers, light flooded the small alley. The door to Catalina's balcony had opened, and her father stepped out from her room.

"What the hell do you think you're doing?" His voice was thick with fury.

Catalina did not attempt to explain. She turned to face the balcony opposite her and prepared to step over when her father grabbed her hand, pulling her back. He shook her with such force, their shadows looked like that of a puppet master and his puppet. Ignacio could see the anger in his face, the red skin of his neck.

"*Por favor*," Ignacio pleaded. "Just leave her alone. I will leave, and never come back. I promise."

Catalina's father looked down at Ignacio and smiled before pushing Catalina down to the alley below. Her head hit the small balcony across from hers, and as Ignacio threw his arms out to catch her, the red flower she was wearing in her hair fell to the ground.

Ignacio rubbed her hands with his. "Catalina," he whispered, but she did not move. The red flowers Ingacio had brought were scattered around her dark, beautiful hair like a halo.

Ignacio held Catalina to his chest, his tears mixing with the red of the flowers and the blood.

fifteen

BEFORE THEY LEFT THE alley, Natalia turned to look at the narrow steps and the two balconies reaching for one another. Without a sound, Death had walked past them toward the street. His scythe, Natalia thought, also seemed to serve as a cane or a crutch. Death supported part of his body with the large wooden snath that held the scythe's blade.

Natalia came up beside Miguel, Conde trotting between them, and nudged his side. "Psst, Miguel," she said in a low voice. Miguel looked over at her, and Natalia started. She hadn't realized how tired Miguel looked. His eyes were beginning to redden at the corners, and his face looked sunken. Had they eaten anything besides the crackers and water Miguel had on the bus? Natalia had been in such a rush she hadn't thought to take along any food, and felt like kicking herself for not even remembering to bring bread.

She looked at her watch. It was almost three in the morning. It had been nearly twenty-four hours since she lay in her own bed, the night Benjamín disappeared playing over and over in her mind. She hadn't bothered to take the covers off her bed or turn on the fan. The sweat had rolled down her face as she tossed, sure she could hear Benjamín calling to her. When she couldn't take it anymore, she had gotten up from her bed and crept quietly across the hall to Benjamín's room. She'd touched his dinosaur bedspread and looked at the stuffed t-rex carefully placed on his pillow. His shelves were covered with paper airplanes, boats, and hats. A cardboard chessboard sat atop a Lotería game set on one shelf. On the table next to his bed, Benjamín had stacked the books he had borrowed from the library. Natalia had smiled; most of them were graphic novels, and almost all of them were about Batman. On their last visit to the library, Natalia had insisted Benjamín take at least two comics that were not about Batman. When it was time to check out the books, Benjamín had rushed up with the two comics he had chosen that were not Batman comics—Batwoman and Batgirl. Natalia had rolled her eyes and laughed, but she had checked them out. At least he was reading books about strong women, she remembered thinking.

She picked up the graphic novel at the top of the stack. *Batwoman: Hydrology.* Natalia felt the tears come to her eyes as she saw the tattered bookmark that was saving the place where her little brother had stopped reading. She flipped the book over and began to read the synopsis. She almost dropped the book as she finished reading. Her mind flashed back to the night Benjamín disappeared. She had been so tired, she didn't get up when she heard the scream. With horror, Natalia had realized that she could have saved her brother, she could have stopped La Llorona from taking him. Without thinking, she had run to Miguel's house to tell him, hoping La Llorona would appear to her in the dark of the night and try to take her too, so that she could get her brother back.

Natalia knew it was going to be hard to get Miguel to believe her, but all she had needed was his friendship. She had known that would be enough to get him to come with her. That, and the thought of being close to the last place his grandfather had been. As she looked over at him, Natalia could almost feel the hopelessness hanging over him, and she wished his grandfather was still alive to help him.

"What?" Miguel asked her.

Natalia blinked. "What?" she repeated.

"That's what I'm asking you," Miguel said. "You called

me."

Natalia snapped her fingers. "That's right," she said, trying to keep her tone light. "I was going to ask, do you think—is Death—do you think its leg is hurt?"

Immediately Natalia wished she could take her question back. Death, who had been walking at the front and off to the right, stopped and turned back to face them. El Charro took his sombrero off and began to fix his hair, then started to busy himself by stroking his horse's long black mane. La Llorona stood off to the side, a curious expression on her face, almost as if she was interested to know what would happen next. Miguel began to shift from one foot to the other, and Conde sat down and began to scratch near his ear. The redness in Natalia's face was visible with only the light of the moon.

"*His*," Death said.

"I—I'm sorry?" Natalia stammered.

"*His* leg," Death said, "not '*its*'. I was a man, once."

Death turned and continued to walk through the deserted street, still leaning heavily on his scythe with the right side of his body. Natalia and Miguel remained silent, neither wanting to even think anything that might be offensive.

When Natalia next looked at her watch almost two hours had gone by. She wanted to ask Miguel if he thought that

Death had forgotten they were following him, but decided against it. As she watched, she saw Miguel pull out the last of his crackers and begin to break off small pieces, tossing them to Conde, who caught them hungrily. When El Charro and La Llorona turned at the crunching noise, Miguel raised his pack of crackers into the air, but they shook their heads. "*Ojalá pudiera*," El Charro said.

"Do you eat food?" Miguel asked, fairly confident El Charro would not get as offended as Death would if he asked him that question.

"Don't you know the legend?" La Llorona asked, rolling her eyes. "He eats hearts. Particularly the hearts of young women." She stared pointedly at Natalia.

El Charro looked at La Llorona sadly. "I haven't eaten a woman's heart in a very long time," he said as Natalia took a step closer to Conde.

Miguel gave the last of the bits of cracker to Conde, then put the crumpled package into his backpack. He took out the bottle of water and offered some to Natalia, who drank gratefully. Miguel bent down to give the last of the water to Conde. The dog lapped it up happily, his tail wagging. As the group went on ahead, Miguel placed the cap back on the bottle and unzipped his backpack, sliding the bottle back inside. If they found a fountain, he could refill it later.

Conde's ears snapped up and he turned to look back the

way they had come. The streets were still dark; the moon had retreated behind the clouds; but it would not be long before the sun would rise. Miguel stared into the darkness, wondering if the roosters would crow here, far away from his grandfather's house. Everything was still until, suddenly, there was a flash of movement. Something white. Miguel raced after it, Conde keeping up beside him. He could hear Natalia behind him. "Miguel!" she whispered in a panicked voice. "Miguel, where are you going?"

There was a clop of hooves as El Charro's horse stopped and turned, but Miguel didn't look back. He didn't want to see Death staring after him. The white blur disappeared down an alley and Miguel picked up speed. He turned the corner just in time to see the familiar white coat. Now he was sure.

"Doctor!" Miguel shouted.

Suddenly Miguel was lifted off the ground and thrown against the stone wall. Conde barked and ran to his side. He forced himself into a sitting position. A dark shadow loomed in front of him, and just as quickly as he had fallen, Miguel was back up against the wall. The blade of the scythe was inches from his neck. Conde barked, then grew silent.

The thick darkness of Death's cloak surrounded Miguel. He couldn't see any of his companions, but he could hear them. Slowly, Miguel was lowered to the ground, the blade still just below his neck.

"The next time you wish to call attention to our group, reconsider." Death turned back down the dark alley.

"But—" Miguel began.

"What could have possessed you to run off like that?" La Llorona asked. Miguel could see her clearly now, floating a few inches above the ground.

"It's just..." Miguel said, "I saw someone. Or something."

Death stopped in his tracks. "Who?"

"I-I'm not sure. Maybe it was just a trick of the night. I haven't really slept," Miguel responded weakly.

El Charro rubbed his chin. "Who is the doctor?" he asked.

La Llorona whipped around to face him. "What did you say?"

El Charro repeated, "The doctor. Who is he?" He gestured toward Miguel. "He called out his name."

Natalia spoke. "The doctor? Your grandfather's friend?"

"Friend." La Llorona repeated. "Miguel, is that who you saw? Is that who you ran after?"

Miguel was not sure. Was it? He thought it was, he was almost sure...but how much sense would that make, anyway? How could the doctor have gotten to the city of Guanajuato from Valle Hermoso so quickly, when they were almost eight-hundred kilometers apart? And why?

Then again, here he was with Natalia.

"I—I thought I saw my grandfather's friend, but it must have been a mistake," Miguel finally said.

"We must move quickly," La Llorona said, looking purposefully at Death. Death stared back at her, and an uneasy quiet settled over the group.

El Charro broke the silence. "Women, am I right? Always in a rush." He chuckled, but Miguel and Natalia could sense how unnerved he was by his laugh.

"The sun will be rising soon," Death said. "We must make it to Mexico City."

"Mexico City?" La Llorona asked. "That is where they are hiding?"

Death shook his head. El Charro and La Llorona exchanged glances, La Llorona's eyes flashing bright green.

"The tlahuelpocmimi don't stray far from Tlaxcala for very long. Finding them in Tlaxcala is the problem. The forests are confusing enough for the supernatural to wander. Who knows what would happen if we were to take these two with us without knowing exactly where we were going."

"Wait," La Llorona said, stepping closer to Death, her hand up in the air. "I thought you said you knew where they were."

"I never said that," Death replied. "I said I would help

you find the boy."

La Llorona stayed quiet, and Natalia could almost see her rewinding the past few hours to verify exactly what Death had said to them. Finally, she seemed to reach the moment she was searching for in her memory, and she sighed. "Are you sure we are not just wasting time? We need to find the vampire that took the boy before it is too late." She brushed a lock of hair from her forehead, exasperated.

"Maria," El Charro said, his voice low, "just listen to what—"

"No!" she cried out suddenly. "You listen! For centuries I have searched, and the kidnappings just continue. They never stop, and they are becoming more frequent. We have a chance to save this boy and catch the vampire that—"

El Charro reached over and grabbed La Llorona's hands, trying to calm her down. "Maria, please, you must be silent. People will hear—"

"Let go of me! Don't you touch me!"

"Maria, please—"

"No! You have no idea! No idea! This vampire took my children and I finally have the chance to get them back and kill the monster that took them—"

"No! No you don't, Maria. They are gone! Our children are gone They have been gone for a long time! You can't keep chasing after them like this, it will kill you—"

La Llorona pushed him away with such force that El Charro fell to the ground. Natalia and Miguel stepped back, their hearts pounding in their chests. Conde trotted over to El Charro, sniffing him carefully.

La Llorona looked down at El Charro, her voice barely above a whisper. "You forget, I died a long time ago."

She turned back to Death. "In Mexico City we will find the help we need to track the tlahuelpuchi that took this girl's brother?" Her voice was almost threatening.

Death nodded once.

La Llorona nodded in return. She motioned for the group to come closer to her. "I will take us there."

Death shook his head. "It is best if I take us there."

El Charro stopped dusting off his pants and held his hands up. "No offense, but your style of travel is not my favorite. I can take us if we need to travel to Mexico City."

"My method is fastest," Death replied.

Natalia and Miguel exchanged glances. La Llorona and El Charro had taken them from one place to another fast enough. How much quicker Death could possibly be?

"We must not waste any more time," Death said, motioning them to move closer to him.

"Remember not to touch him," El Charro said in a low voice to Miguel and Natalia.

"And where exactly are we going?" La Llorona asked,

her voice still cold, but not as loud. "Mexico City is a big place."

Death did not answer. Instead, he merely said, "This will be quick, but I cannot say it will be pleasant."

Natalia and Miguel huddled together, Conde between them. Conde's hackles rose as the temperature dropped.

"Where exactly are we going?" La Llorona repeated.

Death did not move when he answered. "Lake Xochimilco."

"And what could we possibly have to do there?" Her voice began to rise again in anger.

"We must visit the axolotls. They will be able to tell us exactly where to find the tlahuelpuchi."

Natalia and Miguel looked at each other. Weren't axolotls almost extinct? And how could they help?

"The axolotls?" La Llorona repeated, nodding. "They have, if I remember correctly, the ability to grant someone a wish. Someone's greatest desire. In this case, the location of the creature that took Benjamín." She stepped closer to the group.

"Yes. Now, let's go."

"But," El Charro spoke again, "the axolotls, they only grant that wish to one who is—"

Death interrupted him, tapping his scythe on the ground. "Enough! Are you ready or do you wish to stay?"

A cold silence passed between El Charro and Death as they stared at each other. Then El Charro looked over at Natalia and Miguel, his red eyes shining with the first rays of the sunrise. He looked down at the ground and nodded.

The sky became dark as the air around them grew still. For a moment Miguel was surrounded by blackness, an ugly feeling settling in his stomach. He could see his grandfather's shadow in the distance and started to run towards him. Abuelo turned and reached his hand out, dropping his necklace into Miguel's palm.

"Don't stop, Miguel. Don't stop."

"Don't stop what?" Miguel asked, his voice echoing around him. But Abuelo was gone.

Then the darkness disappeared, and he was standing at the edge of a lake. They had arrived at Lake Xochimilco just as the sunrise was breaking through the trees.

Sixteen

"WOW, THAT WAS FAST!" Natalia remarked. Miguel grabbed her arm.

"Natalia, did you see anything?"

"See anything? Like what?"

"Just…anything. In the darkness."

Natalia shook her head. "No, nothing. Probably not enough time. It felt like I just blinked and we were here." She walked away to get a closer look at the edge of the lake.

The feeling in the pit of his stomach had not left Miguel. He felt someone watching him from his left, and turned to find Death standing nearby.

"It's always interesting, the first time you hitch a ride with Death," El Charro's voice came toward them. "So, what is the next step? We call the axolotls?"

Death turned to him. "They only come by the light of the moon."

La Llorona, who was standing near the lake next to Natalia, turned around.

"What? What do you mean they only come by the light of the moon? The sun just rose! Why did you bring us here if they only come at night?"

"The axolotls will know where we can find the tlahuelpuchi," Death replied calmly.

"Yes, but what will we do until nightfall? This is the best plan you could come up with? Waste twelve hours waiting for these creatures? Why didn't you bring us here to begin with? Why did we waste all that time walking with you if you could have just brought us here in seconds?"

"I thought we were being followed."

At this, Death turned to look directly at Miguel.

La Llorona placed her face in her hands. "But you're Death. Are you telling me the best you can do to help us is to have us wait by this lake until nightfall?"

Death nodded slowly.

La Llorona threw her hands in the air. "And...? That's it?"

Natalia walked slowly towards the group, the picture of Benjamín clutched tightly in her right hand, which was balled up into a fist at her side.

"But…Benjamín could die in that time. They could kill him. Drain his blood. Who knows what they're doing to him now? They could be torturing him for all we know!" Natalia's voice rose with every word, until she was almost screaming.

Death lowered his head but said nothing.

Miguel looked at Natalia's face. Somehow she seemed older than she had just the day before. He noticed she wasn't crying, even though her voice was shaking. In the light of the rising sun, her eyes looked almost as red as El Charro's.

Miguel tried to sneak a peek under Death's hood. He thought, perhaps, in the light of day he could catch a glimpse of Death's face. Was it a skull? Would Death's eyes be hollow and dark, black like the night, or would they burn with a fire from Hell—like El Charro's?

For a moment Miguel found himself on the *mecedora* on his grandfather's porch, Abuelo petting Conde and pointing to his deep brown eyes. "You can know everything you'll ever want to know about someone by just looking at their eyes," he had said. "Without even knowing them, you can tell if they are kind and good, or dark and cruel. You can tell if they will be a true friend, or if they will betray you. And you can tell if they need your friendship, based on how much sadness you see in their eyes."

Death's head moved and the hood shifted slightly. Miguel stepped closer, hoping to see anything under the hood that would tell him whether they should trust Death, or whether he was leading them down the wrong path— perhaps intentionally. Why would he bring them somewhere that would not help them until night fell again? What were they supposed to do in the hours they now had to wait? And what would be the other option? To return to Tlaxcala? La Llorona and El Charro could both transport them there within a matter of minutes, but then what? Tlaxcala covered an area of more than four thousand square kilometers, and even though La Llorona and El Charro could transport them from place to place in a heartbeat, Miguel was not sure if they would be able to find Benjamín that way. What if these vampires were holding him underground? How would they know? That would be twice the area they would have to cover. They could possibly split up, La Llorona checking half of the state and El Charro the other, but checking every single part of Tlaxcala would be impossible. It seemed waiting until nightfall to receive an exact location was the most time saving method. What else could they do?

A nagging feeling crept up the back of Miguel's neck, and he couldn't determine whether his distrust of Death was increasing or if another thought was trying to take form in his mind but was not quite making it through.

A white flash through the trees across the lake caught his eye. He glanced over at Death, but Death had not reacted to the movement and was still standing with his head lowered.

"This is ridiculous," La Llorona said. Somehow the quiet of her voice was colder than her screaming. "We can't waste any more time in this place. Thank you for trying to get us a meeting with these magical creatures, but we don't have time for this nonsense. We need to find Natalia's brother. The sooner the better." She turned and strode toward the lake, the lace on the bottom of her dress dipping into the water as she reached the edge. The water began to swirl and Miguel realized it was moving in the same way the water in the canal had moved just the night before. She was controlling the water. But what was she going to do?

"Maria," El Charro began, extending his arm out toward her.

La Llorona lifted her left hand in the air without bothering to turn around.

"Save your breath. You are both cut from the same cloth—heartless, soulless, and filled with darkness. You cannot possibly understand what we are after, and certainly not why. And if you did, you would know why we cannot bear to wait here and do nothing."

The water continued to swirl, but it was as if someone

had turned the sound off. The rustling of the leaves in the soft wind stopped, and El Charro stood, unmoving, with his hand still outstretched. When she looked at El Charro's face, Natalia found that the fire that had burned there before had dimmed. He seemed frozen, and she couldn't even tell whether he was breathing. He became suddenly more transparent than before, in sharp contrast to the crimson red shade that La Llorona's cloak had taken on. She was now only transparent near the water, and Natalia could see the clear liquid through the lace of the cloak.

El Charro pulled his arm back and held it near his chest, and as Miguel watched him, he could almost name what he saw in El Charro's eyes.

Conde trotted to the edge and lapped up some of the water. La Llorona turned and motioned for Miguel and Natalia to join her.

"We must go. There is no help here. We are just wasting time. If we leave now, we will have almost all of the daylight hours to search in Tlaxcala."

Death raised his head and approached them. "And where will you search?"

La Llorona turned back toward the water. "Everywhere," was her only response.

A flicker of flame passed through the eyes of El Charro. Miguel wondered if he was as uneasy hearing La Llorona's reply to Death. Miguel stepped back for a moment, shaking his head. Part of him knew this was not happening, but what would happen to someone who spoke to Death that way?

Death chuckled. It was a strange, awkward sound, almost as if Death was not used to laughing and had forgotten how.

La Llorona turned to face him. "What is so amusing?"

For a brief moment Miguel was certain that Death looked toward him, and he looked down at the ground, wondering if Death had the ability to read minds.

"It is not possible." There was no trace of laughter in Death's tone.

"We have more of a chance of finding Benjamín if we actually go search for him than if we stand here doing nothing."

Death shook his head. "If you would only wait a few hours. The axolotls will be able to identify where exactly in Tlaxcala we need to look. You could attempt to search for him, but if we stay here and wait, we have more of a chance of reaching him before tomorrow's sunrise than if you were to leave and begin your tedious search now."

"But who knows what could be happening to him now? He could be hurt, or worse." Natalia's voice was pleading.

El Charro broke in, "Those hours can seem...almost eternal."

La Llorona looked over at him, but El Charro's eyes were far away, in another time.

Death stepped closer to Natalia. "I know," he said to her. "Believe me, I know about eternity." He stepped so close to Natalia that Miguel wanted to reach out and pull her away, afraid Death's hand would appear from under his cloak and grab her, taking her to some eternal place where he would never see her again.

"We need to wait. The axolotls have never failed. They will find where your brother is being kept. We must wait for them."

"But he could die!" Natalia gasped. "And what then? What will I do if we wait and we are too late? What will I do knowing I just sat and waited while someone hurt him?"

Death was quiet.

"We can go look and, if we are unable to find him or find someone who can help us, we will return before nightfall to meet with the axolotls. That way we don't waste time but we still have the opportunity to meet with them if we need to." La Llorona's voice was firm.

Death gestured toward Natalia, Conde, and Miguel. "How much sleep have they had?"

La Llorona was silent.

"I am sure you met with them as soon as they arrived in the country. And I am also sure they have not slept for some time before that. What good do you think they will do if they spend another half day searching with you? What help will they be to Benjamín? And most importantly, how well do you think they will be able to stand against the tlahuelpocmimi—who have existed for thousands of years—with no sleep and almost nothing to eat except salted crackers?"

Miguel's face reddened. Natalia opened her mouth as if to speak, but then stopped.

"Let them rest here," El Charro said. "Let them rest, we will gather food for them and return, and the axolotls will show us the way to the boy."

Another flash of white across the lake caught Miguel's eye. He had been waiting for it, and now he was sure that something had passed by. No, *someone*.

"But the boy—"

"Is Natalia's brother," El Charro finished. "She should decide what our next step should be. He is her brother."

La Llorona took a deep breath, then nodded, looking toward Natalia.

"You are sure the axolotl will be able to tell us where Benjamín is?"

"If that is what we wish to know," Death replied.

El Charro looked over at Death, uncertainty in his red eyes.

"Will they be able to tell us how to take Benjamín safely from the tlahuelpuchi?" Miguel could tell that La Llorona was still not completely convinced waiting by the lake was the best option, and he could sense the urgency in her voice.

They all looked at Death expectantly. Even Conde sat down carefully, waiting.

Natalia spoke up. "I thought a tlahuelpuchi could be killed with garlic and metal?"

Miguel stared at Natalia in surprise. How long had she been thinking about how to kill the tlahuelpuchi? He tried to think back to the legends his grandfather had told him and his sisters. His grandparents had always had a string of garlic by the front and back doors. But he didn't remember his grandfather ever telling him about metal.

Death looked over at El Charro, who sighed and shook his head. "Sadly, Natalia, it is not that simple. No one who has ever killed a tlahuelpuchi has survived long enough to reveal the secret of how they were able to defeat the vampire. That secret is heavily guarded by the tlahuelpocmimi and their families. Anyone who would ever even attempt to reveal this secret would surely be met with a terrible death."

La Llorona looked at Death and took a step closer to him. "Is this true? Not even you know the secret of what can take the vampires to their graves?"

Death faced La Llorona. "The secret of the life and death of the tlahuelpuchi is well guarded. No one I have encountered in the land of the living or the lands that wait beyond has ever made that secret known to me."

Death looked over at Miguel as he finished speaking.

"And we will be able to ask the axolotl exactly how to kill these vampires?" La Llorona asked.

Death nodded.

"And they will reveal the secret to us?" she pressed.

Death looked at her. "The axolotl will answer any question a person wishes to know."

El Charro turned to look at Death at the same time Death turned to him.

"Still, it would not hurt to have some metal and garlic around, just in case," El Charro said with a forced laugh.

"No, it would not," Death replied.

"But what if…" Natalia began.

"Natalia," Death said, stepping toward her again. He paused, and La Llorona looked at him with a warning look in her eyes.

"Natalia, I do not mean to frighten you with what I am about to say. But believe me, I would sense it if your brother was near death. And right now"—he gestured with his cloak—"I do not sense it."

Natalia was about to speak again, but grew silent. She

nodded, closing her eyes, the dark circles underneath them more visible now that they were in the light of the day.

La Llorona sighed and placed her hand on Natalia's shoulder. "You should rest, then. Here, near this tree. All three of you." She motioned for Miguel and Conde to join them under a large tree a few feet from the lake. Miguel sat down, placing his backpack behind his neck. As Miguel watched, Natalia did the same. Miguel watched her blink a few times before finally closing her eyes, her breathing uneven and her hand still clutching Benjamín's picture.

"We will bring back something good for you to eat. For now, just rest," El Charro said, mounting his horse.

"But what about—" Miguel began to ask.

La Llorona raised her arm. "We don't need to sleep. I think we've forgotten how." She tried to laugh.

"You rest," El Charro repeated as they began to walk away from them.

Death stood looking across the lake before he turned back toward Miguel. Miguel felt a cold wind pass through him, and he wondered once again if Death knew what he was thinking.

"Keep her safe," Death said, before turning and walking away.

Miguel waited until ten minutes had passed. Then fifteen. Then twenty. Finally, when he knew that they would probably not return, Miguel stood. Conde stood up next to him, but Miguel motioned for him to stay. "You wait here with Natalia. I just have to check something."

Miguel began to run around the lake, trying to find a way across, when he saw the white flash out of the corner of his eye.

He turned and looked in the direction it had gone. It was almost near Natalia. As Miguel ran back, he heard Conde stand and growl.

"Wait!" Miguel called out.

Miguel stopped walking. "I know you're there," he said. "I know you're there, Doctor."

Leaves crunched as the doctor stepped out from behind a tree, his white coat still unbelievably clean. Miguel looked down at his own torn clothing, sweaty and covered in dirt.

"Miguel." The doctor's voice was hoarse.

"Doctor," Miguel said, his voice steadier than he had expected it to be. "What are you doing here? What's going on?"

Seventeen

THE DOCTOR LOOKED IMPECCABLE and completely out of place. He walked slowly toward Miguel, who began to back away. The confidence Miguel had felt at seeing the doctor, his grandfather's old friend, started to fade away. He looked over at Natalia, who was now deeply asleep. Conde, sitting next to her with his ears up and alert, wanted to approach, but Miguel motioned to him with his hand to stay.

"Miguel," the doctor spoke. "Miguel, you have to believe me. You have to believe that it is not my fault, I never meant..."

Somewhere in the back of Miguel's mind a thought began to form. Was it the doctor? Had he taken Benjamín? Did the doctor give Benjamín to the tlahuelpuchi? No, no—

the tlahuelpuchi wasn't real. None of this was real. He still believed that. He and Natalia weren't really here by the lake. He was dreaming. He had to be dreaming. And the dream was telling him that the doctor had something to do with it.

"Miguel!" The doctor shook him. "Miguel, are you listening?"

Miguel pulled himself away.

"Benjamín, where is he? Where did you take him? Where is he?"

The doctor shook his head. "No, Miguel. I did not take Benjamín."

"You took him. The blood we saw in your truck. It was you." Miguel backed away, tripping over a tree root.

"No, Miguel, please. I did not take Benjamín. Please, you must listen. I don't have a lot of time."

There was a crack in the distance, and a flock of birds rose up and flew over the trees. The doctor took a step backward, and Miguel could see that, despite his clean clothes, his face was red and dripping with sweat. The shirt under his coat was also soaked in sweat at the neckline. There was silence. The doctor looked around, then walked closer to Miguel.

"What are you doing here? You were following us in the city of Guanajuato, and now you are here. Are you here to take Natalia and me too?"

"Miguel, please. I did not take Benjamín! I did not hand him over to the tlahuelpuchi—I would never! Please, you have to believe me!"

"Why should I? Why should I believe you? What about that blood in your truck?"

"Miguel, I—I am a doctor," he faltered.

"That sounded weak even to me. I know you are my grandfather's friend, but he must not have known what kind of person you really are."

There were tears in the doctor's eyes. "No, Miguel. You are wrong. Your grandfather knew exactly the type of person I am."

There was another crack in the distance, but all the birds had already flown away. Then there was silence.

"Please, you have to listen. I don't have much time, and I need to tell you something your grandfather wanted you to know."

"Something's not right here. I'm not a fool. How did you get here, to Guanajuato from Valle Hermoso? How did you know where to find us?"

Miguel paused for a moment to look around, squinting for any sign of movement among the trees. Could it be possible the doctor could travel the way El Charro and La Llorona could? Or was it possible, perhaps, that a specter was accompanying him in the same way? And if it were—

what if the specter did not have good intentions?

The doctor raised his hands in front of him. "Just listen, please. I will try to answer your questions, so please listen to what I have to say."

"Why should I listen to you at all? You wait until everyone else leaves, until Natalia and Conde and I are alone, to come out from the shadows. Why do you have to hide if you are not trying to hurt us?"

"Miguel, I know who is traveling with you. I am not blind to the fact that more than one person in your group would take my life if they could. And I don't doubt that they could."

"If you say you haven't done anything, why should you be worried about that?" Miguel's heart was racing, and he continued to back away, trying to put as much distance between himself and Natalia. If he could get the doctor away from her and Conde, maybe she would wake up, maybe the others would return and the doctor would be too afraid to try to approach her.

"Miguel, I am more a part of this than I like to admit. I wish things were different—I wish my *life* was different—but there is nothing that can be done about some things. Some things we are born into, and we have to carry with us for the rest of our lives. Some horrors are so heavy, but we have to bear them."

"What are you talking about?"

"If you could just listen and pay close attention—"

Miguel cut him off. "Why should I trust you or anything you say?"

The doctor looked down at the ground, beads of sweat running down the side of his face. He wiped the sweat with the sleeve of his coat. Now that he was closer to the doctor, Miguel could see tiny cuts at the base of his neck, and he wondered whether running through the trees had caused them.

The doctor stayed quiet, and Miguel could see his eyes working, his thoughts moving around in his mind.

"Your grandfather, he gave you something. His necklace. With the bottle."

Miguel reached for his backpack, but realized he had left it at the base of the tree with Natalia and Conde.

"How do you know that?"

"He told me. He told me he was going to give it to you."

Miguel stepped closer to the doctor. His grandfather had told him.

"When? When did he tell you?"

"A few days before he passed away."

Miguel closed his eyes. "Why would he tell you that he was going to give it to me? Did he know he was sick?"

The doctor shook his head. "Your grandfather was not

sick, Miguel." Miguel looked into the doctor's eyes. Tears were streaming silently down his face. "He wasn't sick," he said again.

"Tell me," Miguel grabbed the doctor by the shoulders. "Tell me what happened!"

"It was the tlahuelpuchi," the doctor said in a strangled voice. "The vampire killed him."

∞

Miguel stepped back, shaking his head. "No. No, that's not possible. He had a fever. I saw him, I was there."

The doctor shook his head. "Miguel, you must listen. I don't have much time here with you. Your grandfather and I, we have known each other for a long time. And in that time, the tlahuelpocmimi have been a part of us, a part of me and a part of this land. A long time ago, when your grandfather and I were working for a gentleman, this gentleman's son went missing. He was only—"

"One month old," Miguel finished.

The doctor looked startled. "Yes. One month old. The man never forgot. He was never the same after that. That little boy, he was kidnapped the same way that the others were. The same way Natalia's brother Benjamín was taken. There was a scream—a wail—and then the children were

gone. No trace anywhere on the ground. But of course not."
The doctor laughed bitterly. "The tlahuelpuchi flies from
place to place. There is never any trace of footsteps around
the house where the children have been taken. We tried—all
the men that worked there tried to find him, and as the years
went on, a few of us even joined together when another
child went missing, to hunt for the culprit. We hoped that
maybe we would find the other children as well. But we
never did. But one day..." The doctor paused. "I tried,
Miguel. I tried to help. But one day, your grandfather found
out why I never really could."

There was another pause, and the doctor looked around,
listening. It was quiet. There were no more sounds in the
distance.

"Do you know how the tlahuelpocmimi survive? Do you
know who must keep their secret, who helps them stay
alive?" the doctor asked bitterly.

Miguel did not answer, his eyes widening.

"Their family. They are born into a family that knows
what they are and that is sworn to protect them no matter
what. Do you know what awaits a member of the family that
betrays them? A member of the family who gives away their
secret?"

Miguel thought about El Charro's words. "A terrible
death," he whispered.

The doctor chuckled. "A terrible death," he repeated.

"For decades I have guarded my family's secret, such a horrible, heavy burden for anyone to bear. I distanced myself from them, removing them from my life and becoming a doctor in Tamaulipas, befriending the people of Valle Hermoso, kind people who accepted me and believed me to be a good person. People with good hearts, like your grandfather. I pretended that I was just a regular person, a regular human, not part of a family of monsters. When the disappearances began, it was before I became a doctor, and I was working, saving money. When the young baby disappeared, and your grandfather and the other men began to search, I followed, a horrible feeling in my stomach forming when I heard that no footsteps had been found in or around the home. The boy seemed to have disappeared into thin air. People wondered what could have taken the young boy, but I knew. When another child disappeared, I had no doubt. The sister I had tried so hard to run away from had found me. I told myself I needed to face her, so I searched with your grandfather and the other men, for any signs of the culprit, any sign of the children. When I had been a doctor for some time, another child went missing. This one was older, which was strange to me. We went to search, and that is when your grandfather discovered the dark secret I had kept for so long. We caught a glimpse of the tlahuelpuchi that night. The men had been talking about it for some time, about the legend and how to defeat it. But I knew that metal and garlic were not the only things that were necessary to truly kill a tlahuelpuchi. I wanted to tell them how, but I knew that would mean my death for sure. And a part of me wanted to live—a part of me wanted to flee and become a doctor somewhere far away—to pretend I was normal. But I couldn't. I couldn't leave these people to fight something I knew they could not defeat. Your grandfather and I went into the woods near the home where the child lived, with some of the other men in the group. We became separated, and when it was almost midnight, the moon hidden and the darkness enveloping the woods, a tlahuelpuchi appeared. It looked like a large bird flying overhead, and at first I hoped and prayed that that was all it was. But I knew in my heart what it really was. And I knew that it was showing itself on purpose; it knew me, it was a part of me. I could not run any longer. I turned to your grandfather, ready to tell him how to defeat the tlahuelpuchi, ready to face my death, when your grandfather stepped in front of me. The tlahuelpuchi threw him aside and I threw myself in front of him so he would not be killed. In that moment, my sister smiled at me, and promised me that if I told anyone how to defeat her or any other tlahuelpuchi, she would not only kill me, but your grandfather as well." The doctor stopped speaking, his breathing heavy. When he spoke again, his voice was calm.

"Your grandfather had heard everything. He knew. I was sure he would tell the others when we returned from the woods. But when we reached the group, he just laughed and told the others, 'This doctor can really save lives.' He told everyone I had saved him, but never told anyone we had seen the tlahuelpuchi. I would have died willingly if it meant your grandfather could kill the tlahuelpuchi, but I could not bear the thought of knowing that he—my greatest friend— might lose his life." The doctor choked and began to sob.

"But my sister got him anyway. She came for him." He looked up at Miguel, the tears rushing down his face. He covered his mouth with his hand and fell to his knees, his sobs loud and heavy, his shoulders heaving. "He was ready for her. He always knew she would try to come for one of you, and he waited. That night, the night Benjamín was taken, the tlahuelpuchi was not after him. No, the tlahuelpuchi had always been after Amelia."

Miguel felt a blow to his chest so strong he stumbled backward as if someone had actually hit him.

"What?"

The doctor looked up at Miguel. "The tlaheulpuchi was after Amelia. Your grandfather had sensed it, and he knew for certain when Conde began to act strangely. Once, years after the baby boy went missing, when we no longer worked in the fields together, your grandfather saw a woman walking by the canal behind his house. He thought for sure it was La Llorona. He assumed she was the one that had taken the children. He approached her, expecting her to try to drown him, but he wanted to find the children. But he didn't know—"

"He didn't know," Miguel repeated. "He said he didn't know."

He thought about La Llorona and how Natalia had been so sure that she had been the one that had taken Benjamín. He felt a pang when he thought about how much time they had wasted accusing her of having taken him, and he wondered how many times someone had accused her of having done something so horrible. What must that be like?

The doctor was wiping his face with his sleeves. His voice was soft and low when he spoke. "She appeared to him a few more times after that, so that by the time the tlahuelpuchi attacked us, your grandfather already knew that La Llorona was after the same answers he was."

Miguel thought about the night Benjamín had gone missing. He remembered Conde running endlessly back and forth, panting as he passed underneath the window next to the bed where Miguel was sleeping. He remembered hearing Estela's voice talking to Amelia. Was this true? Could the tlahuelpuchi have been trying to take Amelia, and Abuelo had kept her safe?

Miguel's head snapped up. There was something he didn't understand. "When? When did the tlahuelpuchi try to take Amelia? How is it that we didn't hear anything?"

The doctor smiled unevenly. "The creature had been lurking around your grandfather's house for some time. Conde sensed it. Your grandfather knew this day would come, and that the garlic would not do much to protect him. When you and your sisters arrived this summer, there was an uneasiness in the air. Even I felt it. Late at night, after you and your sisters went to sleep, your grandfather would sit out on the porch with Conde and a small metal stake. A few days before his death, the tlahuelpuchi came. I had been keeping watch a few blocks down for any sign, any movement in the wind. When I finally got there, your grandfather was lying next to the canal, the tlahuelpuchi nowhere to be found. Two trails of blood led from the house to the edge of the water, and I realized your grandfather was not the only one that had been wounded. The cut in his side was deep, and there was no medicine that would be able to cure him completely. I promised him I would not tell anyone he had been hurt, but I knew he did not have long."

There was a rustling in the distance, and the absence of

the wind did not escape Miguel or the doctor. The doctor's eyes met Miguel's, and Miguel saw the sadness inside of them—the sadness that he was sure had made his grandfather befriend the doctor. Abuelo had been right: you can tell a lot about a person from their eyes.

Miguel took a deep breath. "And then the tlahuelpuchi returned."

The doctor nodded. He looked over at the spot where Natalia was still sleeping. "And this time, she decided to attack your grandfather by making sure she did not fail to take a child he cared about."

Miguel shook his head. This couldn't be his life. It was impossible. He looked up at the sun in the sky and closed his eyes. He heard the words coming out of his mouth without feeling himself ask them. "He died from that wound? There was no way…he couldn't have gone to the hospital?" The impossibility of how Abuelo had died made it even more impossible to accept that his grandfather was gone. That he'd been taken far too soon by something that shouldn't even exist. How could there be nothing that would ever bring him back? Suddenly thoughts of Miguel's own life stretched out before him, a life where he would no longer have his grandfather to share his experiences with…

The doctor was right—some things were too horrible.

"I tried—I tried to take him to the hospital. But I knew

he would leave as soon as he could and come back, to try to protect you and your sisters."

"But why didn't he just tell us?" Miguel roared. "Why didn't he just tell us we should leave? We would have gone away! And then he wouldn't have had to worry about anyone being taken, he could've gone to the hospital!"

"It's not that simple, Miguel," the doctor said quietly.

"Why not? What's so hard about that?"

"Your grandfather never would have stopped searching for the tlahuelpuchi. Not when so many children are still missing."

The doctor leaned against a tree, the dark circles under his red eyes making his face look bruised.

"How did you get here?" Miguel asked him.

There was another rustling, this time much closer than before. The doctor straightened. He looked beyond Miguel, toward the trees he himself had come from.

"I am descended from generations of tlahuelpocmimi. That has helped me develop abilities that I normally would not have."

Miguel stepped away from him. "If your sister is the tlahuelpuchi that took Benjamín, then don't you know where she might be keeping him? Don't you know where they live?"

The doctor lifted a finger, silencing him. Miguel heard

more rustling.

"Besides the times I have spotted a tlahuelpuchi in the night, I have not had any contact with my family in years."

"Maybe we could start with the home you lived in before, when you were young. Maybe they are still living there?"

The doctor brushed past Miguel, staring at something in the distance.

"Miguel, there is something else I have to tell you before I go. Something your grandfather made me promise to tell you. And you must listen, because I don't have much time."

Miguel stood straighter, his heart racing. "What is it? How to kill the tlahuelpuchi? Did he figure out how to kill them?"

For a moment the concentration in the doctor's eyes was broken. His voice was sad as he replied, "I'm sorry, Miguel, but I cannot tell you that without risking your life...and theirs." He nodded toward Natalia and Conde.

"But your grandfather made me promise to find you and tell you this. Are you listening?"

Miguel nodded. "Yes, yes, I'm listening. What is it?" He stepped closer, waiting, his heart thumping.

The doctor looked into Miguel's eyes and spoke very slowly and deliberately.

"This is not a dream. You are *not* dreaming. This is all

real. La Llorona, the tlahuelpuchi, everything. This is all real. He knows you will not believe it, and that you will not want to accept it. But it is all real."

Miguel listened, the beat of his heart heavy and deafening. Miguel wanted to tell himself it was all a dream—all of it. But at the doctor's words, Miguel did not find comfort in repeating that to himself anymore. And the doctor's final words were the most crushing blow of all.

"Especially his death."

Eighteen

THE DOCTOR HAD DISAPPEARED into the darkness, the rustling of the leaves muffling the sound of his footsteps as he moved through the trees. Miguel ran after him. He needed to know how to destroy the tlahuelpuchi. He had to find a way to kill the vampire, and the doctor knew how.

Miguel ran around the lake too quickly. How had he made it back that fast? He arrived at the spot where he had spoken to the doctor, and as he thought about calling out to him, Miguel noticed something glowing under the leaves. He kicked them aside and bent down, pulling up the doctor's coat from the ground. Only this wasn't the impeccable white coat the doctor always wore. It was covered in dirt and blood stains, the pockets and buttons torn away. Miguel stood and looked around. The darkness had settled so completely, the only reason Miguel found himself able to see was by the moon's reflection in the lake.

The moonlight…

Miguel turned and ran back toward the tree where Natalia and Conde had been resting. Night had finally fallen and the moon had come out, meaning they now should be able to look for the axolotls. He had almost reached the tree when he stopped. Natalia and Conde were gone. Only Miguel's backpack was left. Miguel kneeled down and picked it up, looking around to see if he could spot them nearby. Where had they gone?

It was eerily silent now. Miguel walked toward the lake, hoping the moonlight reflected on the surface of the water would illuminate him and help Natalia and Conde see that he had returned. A white paper cup floated by on top of the water, and as Miguel reached down to pick it up, he saw something bright swimming in the lake. The golden light moved slowly in the water, getting closer and closer to the surface. Miguel approached the water, squinting to try to see what was approaching. Was it an axolotl? Miguel had never seen one in person, only in photographs in books at the library. As the shape approached, Miguel could see that it was easily more than two feet long. This was not an axolotl.

Before Miguel could back away, the light reached out of the water and pulled him into the lake. Miguel's backpack opened up, his clothes floating away. Miguel pushed the creature back, trying to swim to the surface. The creature began to drag him down deeper into the water, which became darker and darker as they descended. As Miguel looked up at the moonlight, he saw his socks floating up to the surface, and he remembered the necklace his grandfather had given him. There was no way he could lose that necklace. He tried pulling away, but the grip around his neck only tightened. Suddenly another shape swam toward him and slammed into the creature that was dragging him down. He turned in time to see the creature sinking and the figure beginning to swim away. He recognized the brown shirt and pants, opening his mouth to try to yell out, "Abuelo!" Miguel began swimming after his grandfather, but he was too fast. The water became darker and darker as he followed, as if the moon was retreating behind the clouds. The water became so dark he could no longer distinguish his grandfather in front of him. When he began to struggle to breathe, Miguel tried swimming up to the surface, but his body felt sluggish and heavy. As his eyes began to close, the moonlight returned, and Miguel saw a small golden creature swimming toward him. He saw three more creatures appear as he sank down, each one watching him with wide, bright eyes.

Miguel felt the water filling his lungs as he struggled to breathe. When his eyes drooped, he looked around in the dark water, hoping to see his grandfather one last time.

∾

Miguel's eyes snapped open, his heart almost stopping at the sight of a hooded figure standing over him. Miguel caught a small glimpse of clean white bone under the black hood before Death stepped away, turning his back. Natalia kneeled down next to Miguel, a bottle of mineral water in her hand. Conde sniffed at Miguel before licking his face, his fur rubbing Miguel's cheek.

Miguel sat up, his back against the tree, his body aching all over.

Natalia's face had tiny beads of sweat. She handed the bottle to Miguel. "Are you okay?" she asked, her voice shaking.

Miguel nodded. "Just a little sore. I think I slept wrong." Miguel took the bottle and drank thirstily. He handed the bottle back to Natalia, looking around for his backpack. He pulled it open, checking to make sure the socks with the chain were still inside.

La Llorona and El Charro stood side by side, watching

Miguel. Death's back was still turned toward the lake.

"Are you sure you are all right?" El Charro asked, his eyebrows furrowed under his hat.

Miguel nodded, rubbing the back of his neck. "Why?" he asked.

La Llorona looked at him. "For a moment we could not wake you," she said to him. "Was everything well… while we were gone?" she asked Natalia.

Natalia nodded. "We stayed by this tree, sleeping," she replied.

Death turned around. It seemed to Miguel that he was leaning much more heavily on his scythe than before.

"Nothing happened?" Death asked.

Natalia shot a side look at Miguel. "No. I don't think so. We were sleeping."

Death turned his head to face Miguel, who looked away. The sun was setting, rays of red and orange and blue coloring the sky. A slight fog was beginning to set in as the sky grew darker. How long had he been asleep? Had he really been asleep the entire time?

Death was still watching him. Miguel cleared his throat. "The sun is setting."

La Llorona looked up at the sky. "It is beautiful," she said, her voice soft with sadness.

"They brought food," Natalia said to Miguel, handing

him a package wrapped in white crisp paper.

Conde sat next to Miguel excitedly, ready to share. Miguel unwrapped two tacos filled with meat and onions and two filled with beans. He began to carefully remove the onions, not wanting to lift his gaze, afraid Death would still be watching him.

From the corner of his eye, Miguel saw El Charro tap Death with his hand. "*Ya vez, te dije*. Dogs can't eat onions."

Death turned his head slowly. "I know."

"Then why didn't you get the tacos without onion like I told you?" There was a slight hint of laughter in El Charro's voice. "Wait, you don't think that if he eats the onions, he will be protected from the tlahuelpuchi, do you?"

La Llorona rolled her eyes. "Don't be ridiculous. He doesn't think that."

Death remained silent.

La Llorona raised her eyebrows. "Do you?"

"Of course not," Death answered, a little too late. "The onion gives the flavor."

El Charro turned and hid his smile.

"Where did you get these?" Miguel asked.

"There are some food vendors not too far from here," La Llorona answered.

"But you were gone all these hours," Miguel said, unsure where he was headed.

La Llorona nodded. "We let you rest first. We split up and walked around the area to make sure we were not being followed or watched."

"You didn't see anyone?" Miguel asked, immediately wishing he could take back the question.

"No. Did you?" Death said, much too quickly. He adjusted his scythe as he placed more of his weight on it.

Miguel shook his head and lowered his eyes, busying himself with the tacos and sharing his meat with Conde, who gobbled it up eagerly. Miguel ate slowly and deliberately.

Natalia turned as La Llorona made her way toward the water. She remembered with a heavy heart how she had accused La Llorona of taking her brother, and imagined what La Llorona must feel every time she neared water. To know that something so good and pure and beautiful was feared because of you. Natalia found it hard to imagine what that burden felt like. As she watched, El Charro walked over to La Llorona, whispering something in a low voice. He reached over, trying to take her hand, but she pulled away quickly. If Natalia hadn't met them—if her brother had not been taken—and she spotted them standing beside each other as she was walking by, it would be easy for her to think that they were a young couple, enjoying each other's company by the quiet water. She tried not to think of

Benjamín, tried not to wonder what he was doing at that moment, what could be happening to him, whether he was still alive. She looked over at Death, who turned to look at her. She wished Benjamín could be there with her. She knew exactly what he would do if he were here. He would tell La Llorona that she was beautiful, and ask El Charro if he could ride his horse. She smiled as she realized that he would be the one brave enough to ask what she and Miguel were afraid to—did Death have a body underneath that black cloak?

Death shifted his weight. He lifted his head up toward the sky, and Natalia imagined what they would see if his hood would slip off and reveal what was underneath. The sky had turned a dark blue—almost black. As they all looked up at the sky, there was a distant rumble of thunder.

Death looked back down and began to walk toward the lake. "It is almost time," he said.

Miguel crumpled up the paper and drank the last of the mineral water. He was still so sore, and his chest felt heavy. He placed his backpack over his shoulder and began to follow Natalia, Conde by his side. As they gathered near the edge of the water, El Charro's horse let out a soft neigh and tried to back away. Conde let out a soft growl. The sky had grown dark now, and Miguel was not sure if it was now night, or if there was a storm coming.

The air grew quiet around them.

"Don't be afraid," Death said, and Conde and the horse grew still.

Suddenly there was a flash of lightning so bright, it illuminated the sky. Flashes spread out in different directions, and it appeared as if a great hand was stretching its fingers across the sky.

Natalia laughed. They turned to look at her, and her face reddened.

"It's just... it's spider lightning," she said. "Benjamín showed me a picture once, in one of his weather books. I had never seen it in real life."

La Llorona looked at Natalia and smiled. "Very beautiful," she said.

The water began to ripple gently, and four small bright lights could be seen coming towards their side of the lake. As they got closer, Miguel could see that one of them was the same gold as the creature from his dream. The four creatures swam in a line, one behind the other, the golden creature leading the way. They were about a foot long, with a fin extending to the back of their tails, and four short legs. There was another flash of spider lightning, this one spreading across the entirety of the night sky and lingering much longer, so that when it finally faded, it resembled the embers of a dying fire.

The creatures came to a stop in front of the group, lining up side by side, first the golden, then pink, grey, and finally black. Natalia came forward, anxious to find where her brother was being kept. El Charro put his hand up, motioning for her to step back.

"These are the axolotls," Natalia said, her voice urgent.

El Charro nodded. Death walked forward, in front of the group, and bowed. El Charro and La Llorona followed. Natalia and Miguel looked at one another uncertainly before bowing, looking at the axolotls as they did.

They were beautiful. Their bodies seemed to shimmer in the water, almost as if they were covered in glitter. Their eyes were large and shiny, and although they all had deep dark eyes, Miguel felt that each of them was looking at him. Miguel wondered why there were four axolotls, and almost as if she was reading his mind, Natalia whispered, "They're not really found in the wild anymore."

Miguel looked around at the lake, which he knew was much smaller than what it used to be. The axolotls stayed quietly in the water, and as Miguel watched, a paper cup passed by in the water that separated them from the group. Miguel stepped back.

El Charro turned around, slightly lifting his hand to motion for Miguel to come back. The golden axolotl came forward as Death turned and beckoned for Natalia and

Miguel to approach.

"These are the axolotls," Natalia repeated.

Death bowed his head once more.

"These are the axolotls," he replied. "And this"—he gestured to the golden axolotl, who was watching Miguel carefully—"this is Xolotl."

Nineteen

M IGUEL AND NATALIA BOTH took a step back, each one wondering whether they had heard correctly. Did Death really just say *Xolotl*? As in the god?

Death shifted slightly again.

Xolotl floated in the water, the three axolotls behind him also floating quietly. He looked at each member of the group, his shiny eyes moving over their faces and lingering, before he nodded and moved on to the next one. When he reached Miguel, he moved forward a few inches in the water, so that his face was now over the dirt.

Xolotl directed his gaze over to Death and nodded again. "It has been quite some time, dear friend," he finally said. His voice held the same rumble as the thunder which had accompanied the lightning that had marked his appearance.

Death nodded. "Yes, a very long time," he replied.

Because of the axolotl's natural facial features, Miguel could not tell if Xolotl was smiling or not. He watched as the salamander emitted a glow as he breathed, and wondered whether the other three axolotls accompanying him were also gods.

"And you have not grown tired yet?" Xolotl asked.

Death chuckled, but did not answer. El Charro looked over at him, but neither Miguel nor Natalia could read his expression.

Xolotl emitted a bell-like laugh that trilled in the night. "And here I was thinking that was the reason why you were here to see me."

Natalia and Miguel glanced at each other, neither of them understanding the conversation. La Llorona looked back at them, her face full of irritation. She raised her eyebrow at Death.

Death cleared his throat. "Not today," he said, his voice serious.

Xolotl looked at Miguel and Natalia. "I take it this human is the reason why you are here," he mused, nodding slightly at the two. The humor began to fade from his voice.

La Llorona nodded. "Yes. This is Miguel and Natalia," she said, gesturing toward them.

Miguel began to walk forward, but Natalia reached the axolotls first.

As she approached them, she bowed. "Please, sir, I need help in finding my brother, Benjamín. We know he was taken by a tlahuelpuchi, but we do not know where to find them. I have heard that you are able to answer the greatest desire of someone's heart. Could you help me, please?" Natalia was breathless. She still had not lifted her head, and Miguel was certain that she was close to tears. This was it. The axolotls could tell them where to find the tlahuelpuchi. Miguel felt a pang of guilt as he remembered that it was Amelia whom the tlahuelpuchi had wanted to take first, not Benjamín. If she had been taken, it would be Miguel who would be wondering where his sister was, if she was hurt, or if she was close to death. He felt an urge to reach out and place his hand on Natalia's shoulder. The doctor was right. There are some horrors that would be unbearable.

Xolotl looked at Natalia for a few moments, then turned toward Death, and Miguel thought his shiny black eyes had widened. Miguel felt an uneasy feeling in the pit of his stomach. *Please, please don't tell us you can't help*, he thought. What would they do then?

When Death did not speak, Xolotl turned back to Natalia. "It is true. I am able to tell someone the answer to their heart's greatest desire." He stopped speaking. El

Charro had begun to cough loudly and almost uncontrollably. Miguel's eyes narrowed. Did specters cough?

"Ugh, ahem, ack," El Charro said loudly, almost spitting.

"But I can only—" Xolotl began, when Death interrupted.

"Perhaps the boy," Death said fervently. "Please, perhaps the boy. This is urgent. The girl's brother has been missing for some time now. Who knows how long he remains safe."

"But don't they—" Xolotl tried again.

El Charro waved his hand. "Please, Xolotl. We must get to the boy."

Xolotl looked at El Charro, then at Death, and then back at Natalia and Miguel.

He turned to Death once more before saying, "The truth is like a shadow. The sun always rises to reveal it."

Death shifted, readjusting his sheath. He attempted a laugh. "I must be getting too old for this."

Xolotl nodded. Looking at Miguel, he spoke. "What do you wish to know? What is your greatest desire?"

Miguel stepped forward, taking quiet deep breaths to try to slow his heart rate.

"We need to know where Benjamín has been taken by the tlahuelpuchi, please."

Xolotl shook his head. Miguel thought this looked odd

for a creature that looked as if he was constantly smiling.

"No. I will not answer what others want. I am looking for the answer *you* seek."

Miguel stayed silent, not knowing what the proper response was.

"What do you wish to know? If I could answer a question for you, what would it be?"

La Llorona looked at El Charro, who shook his head. She furrowed her brow, but remained silent.

"What do I wish to know?" Miguel repeated.

Death stepped forward, but Xolotl shook his head.

Miguel looked at Natalia. Her face had fallen but she stood quietly to the side while Xolotl asked Miguel questions. Miguel would be lying if he said that what he wanted to know the most in the world was where Benjamín was taken. As he looked at Natalia, he hoped she would not think badly of him for what he was about to ask. But hopefully, she would see that it would lead them to the same destination.

"Where is the tlahuelpuchi that killed my grandfather?"

Death's head spun to face Miguel, but Miguel's heart was beating so fast he did not notice.

Xolotl nodded. "You will find the tlahuelpuchi that killed your grandfather in the Forest of Shadow."

Miguel's eyes widened. "Where is that?"

Xolotl answered, "To get to the Forest of Shadow, you must first pass through the Forest of Light. Once you reach the Forest of Shadow, a guide will lead you to the place where the tlahuelpuchi lives."

Miguel nodded. "Yes, but where is the Forest of Light?"

Xolotl shook his head. "I can answer one more question," he said, his voice wavering. "Are you sure that is the last question you wish for me to answer?"

Natalia watched Miguel, almost seeing the countless questions running through his mind. How was it that Miguel's grandfather had been killed by a tlahuelpuchi? Was that true? And why hadn't Miguel told her? Was that tlahuelpuchi the same one that had taken Benjamín? Could there be two, or were they the same? They had to be, and Miguel had to know that they were, and that the instructions given by Xolotl would lead them to the same vampire.

"I wish to know…" Miguel began, choosing his words carefully. "I wish to know how to destroy a tlahuelpuchi."

Xolotl looked back at the three axolotls behind him for a few moments before turning back to Miguel. His eyes passed over the group once more. Conde stepped forward, trying to sniff the axolotl.

"In one of my transformations I am a dog," Xolotl said, his shiny wide eyes looking at Conde. "Very loyal, this dog." His voice was distant.

El Charro cleared his throat. Xolotl looked back at Miguel.

"How to destroy the tlahuelpuchi? Your grandfather has given you the answer to that."

Miguel shook his head. "No, my grandfather passed away, he didn't tell me anything about how to kill a tlahuelpuchi."

Xolotl nodded. "He gave you the answer."

"But—"

"I am unable to answer any more questions." He looked at Natalia. "May you find your brother." He turned to Miguel. "And may you find peace."

As he began to turn away, he started to glow even more fiercely. He looked like a glowing star in the middle of the lake, far brighter than the moonlight or its reflection.

As Xolotl and the other axolotls began swimming away, he turned back to look at them once more, his shiny wide eyes stopping on Death.

"Perhaps you are getting too old, my friend," he said, before turning away and disappearing into the lake.

Twenty

T HE LAKE WAS CALM as the final ripples trailed behind the axolotls. Miguel imagined his grandfather beside him, and wondered what he would have asked the axolotls had he been given the chance.

Natalia turned from the lake, her voice urgent. She stared at Miguel, her eyes appearing black. "So, we will go to the Forest of Light, and from there we get to the Forest of Shadow, and that is where the tlahuelpuchi is."

Miguel looked confused. "I am guessing it is not literally a forest of light, right?" he asked, hoping Natalia knew where he was headed.

She nodded. "I mean, light in a way."

"I believe—" La Llorona began, but El Charro raised

two fingers casually to his lips.

"I don't think there is a place in Mexico known as the Forest of Light," Natalia said carefully.

"But maybe," Miguel said, "it is the firefly sanctuary, *el Santuario de las Luciérnagas*. Abuelo always said the fireflies come together and light up the forest. Would that count as a Forest of Light?"

Natalia nodded. "It's the only one I've ever heard of, too," she said, her voice excited.

La Llorona nodded.

Natalia's voice grew higher in pitch. "And, it's in Tlaxcala, where the tlahuelpocmimi are all rumored to live! It would make sense that the forest there would lead us to them."

"But," Miguel said cautiously, "what about the Forest of Shadow? Where is that?"

Natalia shook her head. "To be honest, I have no idea. But Xolotl said to get to the Forest of Shadow, we must first pass through the Forest of Light. So it must come after the *Santuario de las Luciérnagas*, right? We should see a sign after we've been there looking around." She sounded uncertain, but shifted her backpack higher on her shoulder, ready to go.

Death stepped forward, beckoning everyone to come closer to him. Miguel had secretly hoped they would take El

Charro's method of travel, a nauseous feeling forming at the pit of his stomach as he stood waiting in the circle. The air around them grew cloudy and grey, until Lake Xochimilco faded into the dark background. Miguel wanted to close his eyes, but forced himself to keep them open. Everyone faded away and in the darkness he saw his grandfather's shadow again, this time closer to him. He began to walk toward him, but a cloaked hand reached out in front of him as the darkness turned to gray. They were surrounded by trees and it took a few moments for Miguel's eyes to adjust. There were a few fireflies flying around, but the forest was still shrouded in darkness.

"Maybe we missed the season when they all light up?" Miguel said, trying to remember when the fireflies were most likely to fill up the forest with their light.

La Llorona lifted her hand up, motioning for them to wait. "It should not be long. They will light up," she said, looking at Natalia, who smiled.

El Charro was trying to calm his horse, who was lifting up his front legs and trying to back away. He looked over at Death, who nodded.

"We will go another way," El Charro said, pulling his horse back.

Natalia's head spun around. "Why?"

"We are unable to enter," Death said.

"Why can't you enter?" Miguel asked.

There was silence. They looked from El Charro to Death and back again. El Charro finally answered.

"I suspect this sanctuary is for those who have a light still in them. Death, my horse and I, we do not."

"It would make sense that we would not find the tlahuelpuchi in this Forest of Light, but instead after we have traveled through it. The tlahuelpuchi probably cannot enter here. You should be safe until we get to the Forest of Shadow." He tried to sound reassuring, but Natalia's eyes widened as he spoke the last few words.

"But by then, of course, we will have joined up with you and can continue on." Death added quickly.

Natalia nodded, but her eyebrows were still furrowed with worry. "But... why can you not enter?" she asked.

Miguel and Natalia looked at each other, both waiting for the answer. When Death did not answer, El Charro closed his eyes, not wanting to look at them when he spoke again.

"We do not have a soul."

"It is no matter," Death said quickly, waving his hand. "We will go around and meet you on the other side," he repeated.

"But how will you know where the other side is?" Natalia asked. "How will you know if we don't take a turn somewhere and end up on a different side completely? How will we know when we have reached a point where we are supposed to meet with you?"

"We will just have to wait and see," Death said, somewhat impatiently. "I am sure we will find each other at the right time."

El Charro took off his sombrero and ran a hand through his hair before putting the hat back on. "Assuming you are some of the only people going in to the forest, we should be able to find you quite easily," he said. "You do, after all, emit a certain light. We can sense that and track you."

Natalia nodded, but Miguel could tell she was uneasy. A part of him wondered whether what El Charro had just said was a lie, but he was secretly glad El Charro had said it, anyway. Looking at Natalia, who had at least partially relaxed, Miguel decided not to ask any questions and just nodded.

The moon had risen higher in the sky, illuminating the trees. Natalia had expected there to be more sound than there was; the quiet of the forest was beginning to unnerve her. A soft wind picked up, moving the leaves of the tall pines. Death and El Charro began to back away, the horse kicking his legs up even more furiously than before.

Slowly, small glowing lights began to appear through the trees, first as lone lights in the distance, then in groups, closer and closer.

"We must go," Death said, and he turned with a sweep of his black cloak. El Charro mounted his horse, tipped his sombrero, and turned, galloping away behind Death and into the darkness.

Miguel looked at Natalia, her eyes filled with worry. "They sure left in a hurry," he said, trying to fill the silence.

La Llorona looked over at Natalia, placing a hand on her shoulder. "There are creatures of light in this forest," she said in a whisper. "They will be much safer if they take a different route."

"What do you mean?" Natalia asked, stepping closer to her.

More fireflies began to light up. Lines of small lights began to move through the trees like glowing snakes. As more fireflies began to rise up from the ground, it almost seemed as if they were about to fall into a universe full of tiny stars.

Conde began to run around, chasing the small fireflies and trying to catch them in his mouth, never quite reaching them. Miguel watched him for a few moments, then turned toward Natalia, knowing she must be wishing Benjamín were here to see this. Was this really happening? Was it possible to have a dream so vivid, one where you sleep and have other dreams? Miguel did not want to believe it, but this dream had gone on so long, he did not know how much longer he could bear it. He wanted to wake up, to know Benjamín was okay, to know that his grandfather was still alive. But what if he woke up and his grandfather was still gone?

Miguel realized Natalia and La Llorona were already walking ahead through the trees, the bright red of La Llorona's cloak sparkling brilliantly and reflecting the light of the fireflies. He saw Natalia and recognized her brisk walk, the one she used when she was ready to get to work. Miguel began to run to catch up to them, Conde keeping up by his side.

The light of the fireflies moved around them, sparkling and glowing, twirling and moving in different directions. Natalia looked up at the top of the trees, the fireflies swimming in the air above their heads. If she squinted a little, she could pretend she was floating in space.

"I can't wait to tell Benjamín about this place," she said, trying to make her voice sound excited. "Maybe we can come back one day. Although he's so loud he would just be pointing at everything," she laughed a little bit before growing silent.

"Do you think he's still alive?" Natalia asked suddenly, looking at La Llorona. Miguel held his breath, wondering what the specter was going to say. He was walking behind them and could not see La Llorona's green eyes underneath her red cloak. The eyes might betray the truth.

La Llorona lowered her head before speaking. "If he was not, Death would know," she said.

The fireflies grew silent and their glows seemed to dim before they continued their flight patterns.

As they walked on, the fireflies seemed to be clearing a path for them.

"It's like they're moving out of the way for us," Miguel said. It occurred to him that perhaps the fireflies were moving out of La Llorona's way, and as he looked at her, he wondered how long she had been a specter, and how long ago she was a human. If she was a specter, he would have thought she would know mostly everything about the spirit world, including how to reach the axolotls. But Death had suggested that. Were there some things she didn't know? What had she been doing during her existence as a specter—looking for the tlahuelpuchi that took her children?

It suddenly dawned on Miguel that, if this tlahuelpuchi was the same as the one that took La Llorona's children, how old was it? And how old did that make the doctor?

Miguel broke from his thoughts as he bumped into Natalia, who had stopped walking.

"Sorry," he said, backing away.

There were three paths ahead of them. There were now thousands of fireflies, all glowing brightly. If Miguel stretched his arm out, he could grab a handful of them. The fireflies went towards each path in equal numbers, brightly illuminating each one. Nevertheless, Miguel could see that there were heavy shadows ahead, and that the trees grew closer together down each path.

He crouched next to Conde and looked up at Natalia, who was also waiting to see what La Llorona would say about the paths. She walked forward, looking down each path in turn.

She came back. "I can't sense anything different about these paths," she said at last. "I can't imagine that these paths would be placed in this forest to trick anyone, or to set anyone off track."

There was a *crack* to the right, and they all turned, La Llorona rising slightly off the ground. Conde growled, then grew silent. There was a slight rustling, then a flash of white through the trees, making its way down the path to the right. The fireflies gathered close together and blocked their way, not allowing Miguel to follow. The doctor? As the fireflies cleared, he saw that there were not one, but two figures running side by side, one smaller than the other, both running with incredible speed and growing smaller and smaller in the distance.

Miguel began to walk down the path the figures had fled through.

"Miguel, wait," Natalia said. "We don't even know who that was. What if they're trying to lead us down the wrong path?"

"Only creatures with or of light can make their way through this forest," La Llorona said slowly.

"So... they were good? Then why were they hiding, and why did they run?" Natalia asked.

Miguel raised his eyebrows. She had a point. Why did the doctor feel the need to run away? He looked over at La Llorona, startled to find her sharp green eyes on him, and he knew why. She had mentioned that the doctor knew more than he was saying, and if she knew how he was connected to this tlahuelpuchi, of course she would never want to see him. Who knows how she would react if the doctor actually approached them?

"Miguel," La Llorona said, "what do you think?"

"Hmm?" He had hoped she would not ask him.

"What do you think we should do? Which path should we take? Should we follow the running figures?" She raised an eyebrow.

Miguel looked from her to Natalia, who was looking at him with wide eyes. He knew Natalia would not want to follow the figures, and if he were her he would not have thought it was a good idea either. But there had to have been a reason the doctor was there. Maybe he had something important to tell them. Maybe he had even decided to finally tell them how to destroy the tlahuelpuchi.

"We should follow them," he finally said.

Twenty-one

T HE PATH WAS ILLUMINATED by thousands of fireflies, their twinkling glow reminding Natalia of the Christmas lights Benjamín loved to put up. They walked on in silence, Natalia and La Llorona side by side, Miguel and Conde behind them. Natalia looked back at the entrance to the path that was growing smaller in the distance, and wondered if they chose the right one, hoping with all her heart that they had.

Suddenly Conde's ears perked up, tall and pointy. His grey fur sparkled in the glow of the fireflies, his big black eyes taking in the full light of the moon. He moved his head towards the left, then towards the right.

Natalia strained to listen. "What is that?"

All she could see were fireflies, but the more she listened, the more she was sure that she could hear whispers. Then she saw them. Small children playing in the trees, running, made up of such a soft light that at first she thought she was imagining them.

She gasped. "There are children," she said, pointing. "There, over there."

Miguel turned to where Natalia was pointing. There were small glowing figures running around in the trees, trying to catch the fireflies in their little hands. Conde's head tilted as he watched them, as if he too could not make sense of these figures.

La Llorona had stopped walking. Miguel and Natalia almost walked into her, and they jumped back as they realized that they had almost walked *through* her.

"They are children," she repeated, stepping closer and off the path.

The children noticed her and stopped trying to catch the fireflies. They ran behind tree trunks and hid, whispering in their sing-song voices.

"Don't be afraid," La Llorona whispered to them. "We are good, we are friends."

Natalia and Miguel looked at each other, not sure if they should follow La Llorona off the path.

"Who are they?" Natalia asked, finally deciding to step

closer.

La Llorona shook her head. "Spirits of children, come to play with the fireflies."

"Do they... do they live here?" Miguel asked. "Are they specters like you?"

"Yes... and no," she answered. "I sense something different about them. They have passed on, and it seems they are just visiting this forest. I have not yet passed on—not completely, at least."

"These are..." Natalia began carefully, "These are spirits of children who have passed away?"

La Llorona nodded.

"They were real children?" Miguel asked, watching all the small figures who were now coming back out from behind the trees. They looked over at the group and whispered to each other, before finally starting to play again. Conde whined and began to walk forward, but Miguel stopped him.

"We don't have time to play right now," he said gently, petting Conde's soft gray fur. Conde sat and watched, shaking slightly from the desire to run out and play. Miguel laughed quietly.

As if woken from a dream, La Llorona turned and made her way back to the path. Her green eyes were dark, and she looked tired. Natalia wondered with a pang whether La

Llorona's children, the ones who were taken by the tlahuelpuchi, could be among these figures. She realized as she began to fall into step beside her that the thought must have occurred to La Llorona as well, which was probably why she had stepped off the path so quickly. Natalia would have done the same. If she thought Benjamín was out there catching fireflies, she would have run after him until she couldn't run any more.

"What happened?" Natalia asked, her voice sounding rough after walking in silence for some time. The fireflies were beginning to slow down, getting closer to the ground and landing on tree branches. "To your children," she added quietly.

Miguel looked up, his heart beating fast at Natalia's question. What in the world had made her ask that?

La Llorona was quiet for so long Miguel was sure she was not going to answer. He believed she would ignore the question, and he began to think of things they could say to break the silence. He looked around and realized there were no more specters of children playing with the fireflies. What time was it? How long had they been walking?

When La Llorona spoke, her voice was cold and dark.

"People often say that I married a man who betrayed me with another woman, and that I drowned my children because that betrayal had driven me mad. As a result, I was cursed to wander the waters of the Earth in search of the bodies of my children, and will not rest until I find them." She paused, looking around, and Natalia thought that she, too, must be searching for the children they had left behind.

La Llorona sighed heavily. When she spoke again, her voice was quiet, almost as if she were talking to herself. "There are some horrors in this world that are almost unimaginable."

Miguel was startled at this, remembering what the doctor had said to him near Lake Xochimilco.

"A very long time ago, so long ago that I have trouble remembering now, I did marry. I fell in love with a man who was not a man at all—he was a demon. You've already met him," she said, attempting a smile.

Miguel dropped back a few paces, feeling as if he were listening in on a conversation between Natalia and La Llorona that did not involve him. When she noticed, La Llorona beckoned for him to step closer.

"It is all right," she said. "We are friends."

Miguel's heart ached when she said that, and he swallowed hard. He quickened his pace to cover the distance he had put between himself and them.

"In his case, of course, the legends are true," La Llorona said, trying to hide her bitterness. "He is, or was, a demon, and he traveled the country to find unsuspecting young women to fall in love with him, young women who could provide him with the one thing he needed to continue to utilize the abilities that come with being a demon."

Natalia shivered. "So his legend is true?" she asked.

La Llorona nodded. "All legends have some truth in them, and in his case, almost everything is true. He would eat hearts."

Miguel shuddered, and he tried to shut his mind off before it began to wonder how that was possible.

Natalia nodded. "And then he met you," she said, continuing the story.

La Llorona laughed. "Yes. And then we met and, according to him, he fell in love." She grew quiet, her mind visiting that once upon a time when she truly believed it.

"He did not eat my heart," she said, trying to forget her feelings. "And I loved him. I believed he had become good, I believed that, since he had been created that way, and he had changed, everything would be all right. And for a time," she sighed, "everything was."

The fireflies had now almost completely disappeared, leaving them only with a few stragglers who lit up their way here and there. If it were not for the moonlight, Natalia and Miguel certainly would have begun to have trouble walking in the darkness, and even the moon was sometimes obscured by grey clouds that threatened to bring rain.

"We had three children, two boys and a girl. And they loved him dearly. But then"—she hesitated—"but then he began to disappear."

"To disappear? El Charro?" Natalia asked. Miguel walked closer to them, straining to hear.

La Llorona nodded, wrapping her red cloak around herself.

"He would disappear for days at a time, never telling me where he was going or where he had been. When he returned, it was always in a terrible state. His clothes were torn and dirty, ripped, and had to be sewn up. His horse was always muddied and tired. Lies and secrets are never good in any relationship," she said, turning to look at Miguel as she said this.

She turned back to Natalia. "One should never allow another to disrespect them, no matter how much you love them. And I didn't. We fought often, never in front of the children, but there was so much anger and resentment inside of me. When I would ask what he had been doing, where he had gone, he would simply shrug his shoulders and continue with his work. It got to the point where he stopped acknowledging my questions altogether. And finally, I had had enough."

Clouds covered the moon, and for a moment they stopped to let the darkness pass. Miguel's feet were aching, and he wished he at least had a watch he could use to look at the time under the moonlight.

As the clouds passed and the moonlight returned, he thought he saw La Llorona wiping her face with her cloak. Her green eyes were not as bright as they had been.

As they kept walking, she continued. "I warned him that if he did not tell me what he had been doing, and where he had been going, the next time he would have to leave the house forever. The children and I could do perfectly well on our own, and I would not accept his blatant disrespect of what I thought we had."

"Did you ever find out? What he was doing, I mean," Natalia asked.

Miguel raised his eyebrows, wondering where Natalia was getting the courage to ask such questions so directly.

"No, I did not," La Llorona replied. "I had my suspicions, of course," she added, glancing at them quickly. "I suspected he had gone back to his old ways, and begun eating the hearts of young women again."

Natalia shook her head slightly, not wanting to believe it.

"I have no proof, but what else could he have been doing? And why did he feel such a need to hide it?" She shook her head. "He left again, that final time," she said, her voice fading away. "He had only been gone one night when it happened. There was a noise outside like a rushing wind, and suddenly I heard the chime on the porch. I thought he had returned after just a few hours, but the house was so still, I felt that something was wrong. When I looked out of the window, I remember seeing the moon, so bright and full, and suddenly I saw a large creature rush by. What really caught my eye was the bright pink beaded blanket, the one I had made our daughter. I opened the door and ran outside, but there was no one there. When I ran back inside to their bedrooms, the children were gone. The windows were open, and they were all gone."

They walked along in silence, neither Miguel nor Natalia knowing what to say, both wishing they could think of something, both wishing something would happen that would distract them from La Llorona's words.

"He came back that night," La Llorona said. "He came back, and I yelled and threw everything I could at him. If he had just been there, if he had just been there he could have saved them. He could have kept them from being taken. He was a demon! He would have sensed if someone had been lurking nearby, waiting in the darkness. He could have prevented it. And he said nothing. He knew I was right. He knew he could have sensed them, whoever they were. He knew that our children would have still been there if he had not been off doing who knows what."

"And he still didn't say where he'd been?" Natalia asked

in disbelief.

La Llorona shook her head. "I told him to leave that night, and to never come back. He promised that he had not gone back to eating hearts, that he was not doing anything wrong, but still he would not say what he had been doing. At the very least, he looked ashamed as he left on his horse. I told him…" she said, her voice breaking, "I told him never to return unless he had found our children. But to this day, neither of us has succeeded in the task. I had not seen him in a very long time until you came along," she said, nodding towards each of them.

"How did you know," Miguel began, daring himself to ask a question, "that the tlahuelpuchi had taken your children?"

La Llorona shook her head slightly. "That took some time to find out. At first, the darkest parts of my mind thought that surely some demon had found us, some enemy of their father's that wanted revenge, and had taken them to hurt us. After that night, I left our home, promising never to return until I found my children. As I traveled through different towns, I began to realize that there were patterns to the disappearances. Children, at least one disappearance a month, and almost always when the moon was out. It did not have to be a full moon, either, it could have been the tiniest sliver of a moon. I realized that usually babies and small children were targets, rarely older children or adults. On my journeys, I began to learn just how big the world of the supernatural was."

"You were alone all that time?" Natalia asked.

La Llorona nodded.

"What led you to the tlahuelpuchi?" Miguel asked.

She turned back to look at Miguel before answering. "I began to hear rumors of an ancient type of vampire that fit many of the characteristics I was looking for: they would take young children, usually at least once a month, almost always when the moon was out. It took some time, but I finally saw one, when a small baby, about one month old, was taken."

She looked at Miguel, her eyes shining brightly.

"One month," Miguel repeated.

"One month," she said. "Some time after that, I saw one not too far from where your grandfather lives, in a wooded area." She turned back to face the path.

Miguel wondered if she had been there when the doctor had revealed his secret to Abuelo.

"I had been wandering the country for so long, I had forgotten just *how* long. I have never really been able to determine whether I was given eternal youth and spared death so that I could find my children, or if I was truly cursed to wander the Earth like this forever. But, I never passed on. Perhaps I should ask Death about it one of these days," she mused to herself.

"I decided to approach your grandfather on one occasion," she continued, looking over at Natalia. "Miguel's grandfather had begun to look into disappearances of children as well. Before he really knew about the tlahuelpuchi, I had tried to come to him to tell him what I knew of the disappearances, but like so many others," she looked at them pointedly as she said this, "he knew I was La Llorona and thought I was connected to the disappearances. I had no choice but to leave, very much disappointed."

"And then?" Miguel asked.

"As you know, your grandfather continued his search and began to learn things about the tlahuelpuchi. I felt we could work together to try to find them and destroy them. I believe he had realized what I really was towards the end," she said, pausing. "He was a very brave man," she added, looking at Miguel.

"Your grandfather was hunting the tlahuelpuchi?" Natalia asked.

Miguel nodded, not wanting to meet her eyes.

Natalia's eyes were wide with questions, but she did not ask anything else. Miguel felt a pang of guilt at not having told Natalia what the doctor had told him. A part of him, a deep part that felt buried underneath the hollowness in his chest, wanted to take her aside and tell her everything. He felt nauseous thinking about it, and his selfish half wanted to unload everything, to have someone else bear it, at least for a little while. But looking at Natalia—at her eyes—he felt ashamed. If he had been in her place, his eyes would have been filled with sadness, with anger, with a feeling of betrayal at the secrets around him. But all he saw in her eyes was the deep, dark shade of courage and the light of hope.

The fireflies had almost all stopped glowing, with only a few lights floating here and there. The path had grown dark, and Natalia and Miguel strained to see through the darkness and the thick, tall trees. Miguel walked closer to Conde, his soft fur brushing against Miguel's pants. Conde's eyes glowed in the darkness, as wide and alert as when he was a small puppy. Miguel's heart ached as he wished he could go back to the time when he was visiting his grandfather, when Abuelo first came home with Conde, his soft brown fur sticking out all over. Abuelo had laughed and said Conde needed a good bath and haircut, and Conde had wiggled furiously, almost as if he understood. Conde had chased the baby chicks until the hens had pecked at him and chased him away, and he had finally settled under a tree in the garden, watching the baby chicks play, his eyes hoping they would come close enough so he could play too. He remembered Abuelo's hearty laugh as he had shaken his finger at Conde, telling him he was lucky the gallo hadn't been the one that had chased him away. Miguel looked into Conde's eyes, a small glow reflected in their darkness, wondering what his eyes would betray. Conde looked up, seemingly reading Miguel's thoughts, the small specks of gold inside visible as he turned to look toward Miguel. Miguel bent down to stroke Conde's head, trying to figure out what was in Conde's eyes that looked so familiar. As the last fireflies dimmed their glow, Miguel realized it was the happiness he always saw in his grandfather's.

Twenty-two

T HE DARKNESS ENVELOPED THEM quickly, until all Natalia and Miguel could see was the red of La Llorona's cloak. They stopped walking, Conde stepping forward and letting out a low growl. La Llorona's cloak shifted as she lifted her arm.

"What is it?" Natalia whispered, talking to La Llorona and Conde at the same time.

"I've never seen a night so dark," La Llorona said, looking up at the moon, which had retreated behind the dark grey clouds. In the distance, there was a soft rumble of thunder, and Miguel wished Xolotl could have accompanied them. If he had been able to come in his dog form, that might have even been better. A god like that could have helped them pass through these forests with no problem, and maybe even helped them once they reached the tlahuelpuchi. He still did not know what the axolotl meant when he'd said that Abuelo had given him the answer of how to defeat the vampires.

"Hopefully it doesn't rain on us," Miguel said, trying to think of something to add to the silence.

"The clouds do not seem to be moving," La Llorona said, still looking up. "We will have to continue without the guidance of the moon."

Natalia nodded. "You should walk ahead," she said to La Llorona. "We can see your cloak very well even in the darkness. It can help guide us."

La Llorona began to walk again, her cloak rustling as she walked.

Miguel walked close to Natalia, Conde trotting along beside him.

"Why do you walk?" he asked. "Wouldn't it be easier, or less tiring, to float?"

La Llorona turned her head slightly to look at him. Moments passed, and Miguel began to wonder whether what he had asked had been offensive.

"It helps me remember," she finally answered.

"Remember?" Miguel repeated. "How to walk?"

There was another pause. "What it was like to be

human."

Miguel grew silent, and soon the only sounds were the rustling of La Llorona's cloak on the ground and Conde's soft panting as he walked along beside Miguel.

The moon still did not appear from behind the clouds. As they continued on, Miguel got the odd sensation that they had turned around somehow, that they were heading the wrong way. La Llorona began to slow down, her head turning to the left and the right.

"Something doesn't feel right," Natalia said, giving voice to Miguel's thoughts.

Conde began to sniff the air, his wet snout glistening slightly in the darkness. The forest grew still, and Conde turned sharply to the right, taking a few steps forward. Miguel reached down to grab him, his hand freezing in mid-air. A small light had begun to glow through the trees ahead on the right. Conde took a few more steps forward, then stopped, looking back at them and waiting for them to follow.

"I—I think he wants us to follow," Natalia said, her voice low.

"But…what is that?" Miguel asked. "It can't be a firefly."

Natalia shook her head. "No, but the forest is good, isn't it? I mean, it can't be bad, whatever it is."

La Llorona had stepped in front of them, her head tilted

as she watched.

Standing behind the group, Miguel almost let out a slight laugh at the soft outlines of La Llorona and Conde tilting their heads in the same manner, but stopped himself.

As the light flickered, Miguel realized that it was a flame.

"Is that a candle?" he asked softly, stepping forward.

"I think… I think it's a lamp, or a lantern," Natalia said, squinting her eyes.

As the flame grew, Miguel stepped back. Illuminated in the glow was the profile of a woman in white.

"Who is that?" he asked.

The woman was not facing them, and as they watched, she abruptly turned and began to walk away from them.

"I don't believe it," La Llorona said, beginning to follow the woman.

"What?" Natalia asked.

For a moment Miguel wondered if this was the real La Llorona, the one from the legends that did actually drown her children. From where they were, he could see that the dress the woman wore was white lace. Was this the woman the legend was built upon? But if she was, how was it that she was here in the Forest of Light if only creatures of light could enter? Maybe they had walked in the wrong direction and had left the Forest of Light behind, and were now in the Forest of Shadow.

"Miguel!" Natalia was whispering his name in the dark, and as Miguel shook himself awake from his thoughts, he realized he was falling far behind. Conde had stopped to wait for him, but Miguel could tell he was anxious to follow the woman, who had already advanced considerably.

La Llorona was taking long strides to keep up, and as Miguel caught up, he asked, "Who is that?"

"*La mujer del candil*," La Llorona answered.

Miguel shook his head. "But that legend comes from Guerrero," he said, catching his breath. "I thought she would only appear in that state?"

"Why is she here?" Natalia asked. "So far from her home?"

La Llorona quickened her pace. "To help us."

La Mujer del Candil

THE WOMAN WITH THE LANTERN

LONG AGO, MANY TRAVELED to the Mexican state of Guerrero to visit a shop owned by a woman named Lucero. Lucero made the most beautiful candles in colors people had only dreamed of. Travelers purchased candles for themselves and as gifts for others, and always came back thanking Lucero for the sweet-smelling candles that, like magic, lasted months and months. Lucero worked long hours every night, pouring her love and her soul into each candle she made, knowing each one would get her closer to her dream.

Lucero loved her home, and while she sometimes set off on foot to visit the neighboring towns, there was one place she wanted to visit above all others: la Ciudad del Vaticano, where she could visit St. Peter's Basilica and the Sistine Chapel to leave one of her candles as a gift. Every night, Lucero would take the coins she had earned from selling candles during the day and keep only what she needed to buy food, water, and materials for her candles. The rest, she stored carefully in a red velvet bag she kept in a wooden box in her bedroom. When the bag was full and heavy with the weight of the money inside, she knew it was time to set off on her travels.

Lucero traveled to the village square with some of the last candles she had left, giving them to shop owners and asking that the candles provide them with a guiding light always. She kept three candles: a white candle, which she would use in her lantern as she walked through the village, and two rose-colored candles that she knew would make beautiful gifts. The day she was to depart from Mexico forever, she rose early, before the sun had come out to light her way, and gathered her few belongings and the red velvet bag that held her life savings.

Lucero did not know that, while there were many in town who loved her candles and knew there a magic surrounding her, there were others who only saw Lucero's success as a candle maker. Whispers had traveled through the town of Lucero's departure, and men began to lurk in the shadows on the road to the village, hoping to cross paths with Lucero and the fortune she was rumored to be carrying with her. As she started to walk down the dark road, she relied on the candle in her lantern to see her surroundings. As she passed underneath the tall trees, her feet crunched the leaves that had fallen to the ground, breaking the silence of the night. The shadows around her began to shift, and it was soon clear that she was not alone. Lucero quickened her pace, tightening her grip on the small red velvet bag, the *clink* of the coins suddenly dangerously loud.

As Lucero walked down the dark path, the men came out of the shadows and surrounded her, the lantern falling to the ground as the men stole Lucero's money, her dreams, and her life. The candles rolled out from the bag and the lantern, coming to a stop near the body of the woman who had given them life. Lucero's spirit continues to wander, searching for the men who took everything from her, and for any who may cross her path who have ill intentions in their hearts. And for those unlucky enough to lose their way and find themselves wandering in the dark, she provides the light from her lantern so that they will find their way safely home.

Twenty-three

M IGUEL TRIED TO GET a better look at the woman, but all he could see was her white dress moving quickly through the trees.

"She guides people," Miguel said slowly, trying to remember what his grandfather had told him. "She helps people who have lost their way with her lamp."

"That's right," Natalia said, nodding. "Someone wronged her and she has remained to help others who need to be guided in the dark."

"Yes. A vengeful spirit to those whose intentions are to do wrong, but a good spirit for those who are lost," La Llorona said.

"So that means," Miguel said, "that we went the wrong

way? Back there, through the trees?"

"We must have," Natalia said. To herself, she added, "It felt like something was off."

"Yes, it did," La Llorona said, looking back. "Conde sensed it as well, but I could not sense any other path than the way we were walking, so I went on."

They grew quiet, each of them concentrating on keeping up. The woman was getting further and further ahead, and as they began to fall behind, the light from the woman's lamp began to dim.

"No!" Natalia called out. "Wait!"

They began to run, La Llorona switching from walking to floating.

"*Espere por favor!*" La Llorona called out.

As the moon began to come out from behind the clouds, they realized the woman had led them to a small clearing in the trees. As her light dimmed, she turned to look at them. Her face was hidden in shadow, even with her lamp held high in front of her. As the light of the moon shone down on her, Miguel's heart began to pound. The woman was looking at them, and in her eyes, all he could see was sadness.

"I cannot help you from here," she said, her voice echoing around the small clearing.

As her light dimmed, Natalia rushed forward, trying to

reach her.

"*Muchas gracias, Señora! Muchas gracias!*"

Natalia reached out her arm as the woman faded away, the woman's thin arm reaching back to grab hers as she disappeared.

Conde began to sniff around near the trees, his gray hair shining silver as he moved. With the moonlight back, they could see the clearing well, but the trees beyond were still shrouded in shadow.

Miguel looked around, but it appeared as if they were still in the same forest. The woman had said she could not help them from there. Did that mean that the Forest of Shadow was nearby?

"Do we keep going?" Natalia asked, her voice a mixture of hope and uncertainty. Miguel could almost feel her impatience in the air, the anxiousness of wanting to reach Benjamín.

"Should we keep going the way we were walking, just straight ahead?" Miguel added, wanting them to keep moving.

La Llorona sighed. "As much as I would like to continue," she said as she turned to look at them, "I think this is the point where we are meant to stop and wait."

"Wait?" Natalia asked.

"For Death and El Charro."

Natalia shook her head in confusion.

"We cannot enter the Forest of Shadow without them," La Llorona said. She stepped closer, lowering her voice. "I cannot sense which one of these trees indicates the entrance, so it is best we stay together near the center."

Conde lifted his ears and turned to look at La Llorona, who beckoned to him, and he quickly ran to join them in the center of the clearing.

"But, why can't we enter without them?" Miguel asked, wanting to ease the anxiety in Natalia's eyes. "What if they are already in the forest? We have no way of knowing if they have already passed."

"They would have waited," La Llorona answered. She looked around before moving closer. Lowering her voice, she repeated, "We cannot enter without them. We have souls, and they do not. We need them to be able to enter." She looked at Miguel and Natalia, as if considering whether to continue. In the light of the moon, as young as La Llorona looked, Miguel could see the eyes of a caring mother, and he thought with guilt of the note he had left his own mother.

La Llorona sighed deeply before continuing. "The Forest of Shadow is full of soulless creatures. We must be very careful as we travel through it." She paused and covered her mouth with her hand, considering her next words carefully.

"The Forest of Shadow will take advantage of any opportunity to betray you. Carefully consider your thoughts, your words, and what is in your heart as you travel through it. Many good men have lost themselves forever in this dark place."

Natalia and Miguel nodded.

La Llorona motioned to the ground. "Sit and rest while we wait. They cannot be long now, especially with that horse." Miguel could tell she was trying to lighten the mood, but the caution in her voice filled her green eyes as she turned away from them.

Miguel sat down on the grass, placing his backpack behind him and beckoning for Conde to sit next to him. Natalia sat beside Conde, stroking his fur gently.

Miguel's eyes were beginning to feel heavy, and he rubbed them to try to keep them open.

"You can rest," La Llorona said to him. "Just lie down and close your eyes. We will not leave you behind."

Miguel nodded, then placed his head gently on his backpack. He was almost asleep when there was a crack nearby. Miguel sat bolt upright. The moon was almost completely hidden behind the clouds once again, and as the last of its light began to fade away, he saw that he was completely alone in the clearing.

He stood and reached down for his backpack, but it was

gone. Looking around, he began to feel panicked. They would not have left him alone. They would not have gone to the Forest of Shadow without him, would they? Of course not. But then, where was everyone? What if something had happened to them while he was asleep?

Miguel took a deep breath. No, they were probably in the forest, among the trees, talking, trying not to wake him. He looked into the forest on all sides as he walked around the clearing, but he could not see anyone; there were no silhouettes of hooded figures. Suddenly Miguel heard another branch break underneath the weight of someone's foot. He jumped behind the nearest tree and crouched down. As he listened, two figures approached, their low murmurs traveling through the air.

Miguel strained to hear what they were saying, and as the voices got even closer, he caught the words "Benjamín" and "death." Miguel stood up slightly to see who was coming, and as they approached, Miguel heard the hooded figure speak. "Do not tell Natalia."

Miguel started to back away as he realized Death and El Charro had finally arrived, the horse trailing behind. As he took a step backward, Death looked right at Miguel, straight into his eyes. Miguel stumbled as he realized that Death was not wearing his hood; his face was a pale, white skull, and where his eyes should have been was a deep, never ending darkness.

Miguel tried to stand to walk back toward the clearing, but his feet had become so heavy. He heard another crack and stopped trying to get up. He turned slowly, expecting to see Death standing over him. He jumped back as the moonlight shone on a colorful creature in front of him. With the bright yellow and blue body of a dog, the white head of a rooster, and the red wings of a dragon, the creature easily stood more than six feet tall. Miguel moved back slowly, not wanting to startle it. Was he still in the Forest of Light? Was this a good creature?

The rooster's head moved down slowly and pushed something towards Miguel with its beak. The white object rolled towards Miguel and stopped as it bumped into his foot. Miguel looked closely and reached over quickly to grab it. His socks! The socks that held his grandfather's necklace!

"Your grandfather gave you the answer," the creature said in a thundering voice.

Miguel held the socks close to him as he returned his gaze to the creature. The answer? It bowed its large head and began to turn away.

"Wait!" Miguel called without thinking. He looked around quickly, trying to find Death, El Charro, and his horse nearby, but found he was alone with this creature.

"Wait," he said again, more softly. The creature turned

to look at him. "Who… who are you?"

The creature nodded. "I am an alebrije," came a strong voice. The wings flapped and a gentle wind started up. "I help to guard against nightmares." The alebrije stepped closer to him and flapped its wings more strongly. "And it is time for you to wake up."

The wind from the alebrije's wings was so strong Miguel was blown to the center of the clearing. As he sat up and rubbed his head, he looked up to find six silhouettes standing over him, blocking out some of the moonlight.

"You slept like a rock!" Natalia said, shaking her head and moving away. "Come on, we're ready to go." Everyone backed up as Miguel stood up and gathered his backpack, looking around for any sign of the alebrije in the trees. Had he dreamed the whole thing?

He unzipped his backpack and felt inside for the rolled-up socks that held his grandfather's necklace. Was the alebrije referring to the necklace? Was the necklace the answer to the question he had asked Xolotl?

As he zipped his backpack, Miguel saw Death watching him, and an image of Death's face from his nightmare passed through his mind. Almost as if he saw the image as well, Death turned his head and walked away, leaving the memory of the conversation Miguel had overheard in his dream hanging in the air between them.

Twenty-four

E L CHARRO AND HIS horse stood next to Death in front
of a cluster of trees. Conde lowered his head to the
ground, looking ahead to the forest. Natalia was shifting
from one leg to the other restlessly.

"Well?" La Llorona asked impatiently.

El Charro looked back at her, allowing his eyes to linger
long enough so that she turned away.

He nodded. "This is the spot," he said finally, his horse
tapping his leg on the ground three times as if to confirm
what El Charro had said.

Death nodded as well.

El Charro turned. "We must be very careful as we travel
through the Forest of Shadow," he began, echoing the

words La Llorona had said to them.

"I have already warned them of the dangers of this forest," La Llorona said.

"It bears repeating," El Charro said. Looking at Natalia and Miguel, he continued. *"Este bosque es traicionero,"* he said, lowering his voice. "You will not even realize when it begins to betray you. You must remain alert at all times." He turned and reached for his horse's reins, pulling him gently to his side.

As El Charro and Death started to walk forward, the trees began to groan and shift. The leaves began to twist into vines and wrap themselves around the trees, and there was a loud *crack* as they began to bend over, forming an arch. As the clouds moved in front of the moon, the shadows cast on the trees began to give them a skeletal appearance, so that it seemed like the arch was made out of long, thin, twisted bones.

As they walked through the archway, the wind picked up, the clouds completely covering the moon. They had all just made it through when the trees began to twist and groan once more. The vines released their hold on the trees and shrunk back into leaves, the trees returning to their places side by side.

El Charro and La Llorona glanced at each other, then quickly looked away.

"There's something you don't see every day," Natalia said, trying to lighten the mood.

Miguel laughed, and Death turned his head toward him. All Miguel could imagine now was the skull underneath Death's hood, and he quickly cleared his throat and grew silent.

El Charro laughed, too loudly. "Yes, I am sure that is not something you would see every day." He turned and continued walking, but stopped when Natalia and Miguel began to fall behind.

"It is almost completely dark, and the clouds do not look as if they will be moving off anytime soon," La Llorona said, looking up.

El Charro glanced around, kicking small branches with his boot. Reaching down, he picked up a thick branch, almost two feet long, and held it up.

"This should be fine," he said, mostly to himself. He looked back, his eyes uncertain.

"Go on," Death said, "I am sure before the night is over these two will have seen much worse."

La Llorona turned away, looking into the darkness between the trees, and for a moment Natalia thought she saw sadness flicker in her eyes.

Turning away from them, El Charro moved into the darkness and, taking a deep breath, blew deeply. His skin began to glow a fiery red, tightening over the bones of his face until the sharp edges of the bones were visible, almost beginning to cut through the skin. A bright flame escaped from his mouth, lighting up the top of the branch. As Miguel and Natalia looked at the torch, their eyes landed on the hand holding it. El Charro's hand was now a fiery red, with long black nails and bent, crooked fingers. They turned away before El Charro caught their eyes, and when they next looked up, El Charro's skin had returned to its normal shade, almost transparent next to the flame.

"That should help," he said, turning to look at them. Miguel and Natalia nodded, almost too eagerly.

A deep rumble of thunder rolled through the sky, this time much closer.

"We need to hurry," La Llorona said, "otherwise the torch will soon be extinguished by the rain."

"We must tread carefully," El Charro said, lifting the torch higher as he continued to walk. "We do not even know where we are going, or in which direction we are supposed to go. We must be vigilant."

As another rumble of thunder traveled overhead, they all quickened their pace.

They continued to follow a path straight ahead as they walked, the rumbles of thunder becoming more and more frequent.

"Everything looks the same," Natalia said, her voice nervous. "In the Forest of Light, it seemed as if we were traveling in a straight path, but we ended up going the wrong way. How do we know we are not going the wrong way now?"

El Charro shook his head. "We do not. And in this forest, there is no way to know which way is the right way."

Conde's nose rose high in the air as he sniffed.

"What is it, Conde?" Miguel asked, bending down next to him.

Conde let out a small whine, then began to run off to the side, trailing off of the path they were walking.

"Wait, Conde, wait!" Miguel said, running after him.

"No!" El Charro yelled, his voice coming out like a growl, his skin momentarily glowing red.

He lifted his hand, stopping Natalia from following Miguel. "Do not stray from the group."

Turning, he ran after Miguel and Conde, his torch lighting up the darkness.

Miguel was crouching over Conde, who was digging vigorously.

"We need to return to the others," El Charro said. "Come, Conde."

Conde stopped digging and moved back toward Miguel. There was a white piece of cloth sticking up through the dirt. Miguel's throat tightened as he bent down to grab the cloth, pulling up with both hands. He fell backward as the cloth came up from the ground, throwing chunks of dirt into his face.

Miguel sat up, clutching the coat in his hands.

"Is it his?" La Llorona's voice came from behind Miguel. "Is it the doctor's?"

Miguel could not speak. It was the coat from his dream—the dirty, torn coat—but it was unmistakably the doctor's coat. He nodded.

In the darkness, Miguel did not see Death right away as he crouched down next to him. Reaching over, he grabbed the coat with a cloaked hand.

"Is he okay?" Miguel asked, his voice small. "Is the doctor okay?" He could not remember a time when he had not seen the doctor without his coat.

Death handed the coat back to Miguel, then pulled himself up with his scythe, turning away to look into the darkness.

"The doctor," he said finally, "is no longer part of this world."

Twenty-five

A LOUD CLAP OF thunder broke the silence as a flash of lightning lit up the sky, momentarily casting light on the dark forest. The trees were endless. They made their way back to the path.

"Are we sure this is the path we were on before?" Natalia asked.

El Charro sighed before answering. "To be honest, no. Everyone moved from the path, so it is difficult to know exactly where we were. But, this seems to be about the same distance, from what I can remember."

"What do you think… what do you think happened to the doctor?" Miguel asked.

El Charro and La Llorona looked toward Death, as if

assigning him the task of answering.

Without looking back, Death said, "He has passed on."

"Yes, but, what happened to him? Was he killed?"

"It appears that way," Death answered without stopping.

"By who?" Miguel had tried to keep his voice level, but his words broke as he spoke them.

Death stopped walking, turning slowly, his right hand holding on to his scythe.

"I think you know," he said.

"The tlahuelpuchi? But—but why?"

"Can you think of no reason?" Death asked, turning back to continue walking.

Natalia reached over, placing her hand gently on Miguel's, which was still clutching the white coat, but he pulled away. Miguel wanted to ask Death what he meant, to tell him to answer his questions properly, not with other questions.

Conde's ears perked up as a low trill travelled through the trees. El Charro stopped walking, lifting his torch as high as he could reach. The trilling came again, this time sounding closer. La Llorona joined Death and El Charro in surrounding Miguel, Natalia, and Conde.

"What is it?" Natalia asked, her breathing heavy.

There was silence as the specters looked up to the sky, trying to find something.

Another trill sounded through the night, this time right above them. As El Charro lifted his torch once more, they saw what looked like a large owl flying through the sky, its wings impossibly large.

"A lechuza," La Llorona said, trying to find signs of another.

"What is it doing?" Miguel asked, losing sight of it above the trees.

"Probably giving away our location," El Charro said, looking about at the darkness. He walked around the group, moving his torch into the trees, trying to see if something was hiding just beyond the reach of the fire.

"At least we know we are going the right way," Death said, starting to walk again.

"What do you mean?" Natalia asked.

"It is probably flying back to the tlahuelpuchi, and if it is, then we will simply follow it and soon find the tlahuelpuchi ourselves."

Natalia nodded, quickening her pace.

"Perhaps we should extinguish the torch," La Llorona said slowly. "It must be what gave away our location."

El Charro shook his head. "It is not the torch that did it," he said. "It is the presence of something that is not usually found in this forest." He looked at La Llorona, Natalia, Miguel, and Conde in turn. "Putting out the torch would only make us more vulnerable, since Natalia and Miguel would not be able to see at all in the darkness. If we were to be attacked, we would not have the advantage."

Miguel kneeled down, stroking Conde gently. He was looking around restlessly, panting softly. Death approached them slowly, his head bent down to look at Conde. Gazing at the trees surrounding them, he turned and began to walk forward once more.

"There is something nearby," he said calmly. "Conde also senses it. It is not friendly."

Miguel looked over his shoulder at the darkness they were leaving behind, wishing El Charro were walking at the end of the line instead of the front. It would help to have a demon at their backs.

The dark clouds completely covered the moon, the rumbles of thunder directly on top of them now.

"At least we can see with these lightning flashes," Natalia said, looking up as another bolt of lightning lit up the sky.

A loud crash of thunder seemed to open up the sky. The clouds covering the moon began to break apart, finally allowing the rain that had been waiting to fall to the ground. Miguel reached into his backpack and took out one of the shirts he had brought along, unbuttoning it and placing it gently over Conde, tying the sleeves like a bandanna around his neck. Conde looked up and licked the water running down Miguel's face, and Miguel wished more than anything that they were back at his grandfather's house, sitting on the porch and watching the rain fall.

He reached into his backpack again, pulled out a pair of pants and another shirt, and offered them to the others.

"I am okay, thank you," El Charro said, waving the clothes away. Death and La Llorona shook their heads, and Natalia had already brought out a sweater with a hood to cover her head.

"What about your horse?" Miguel asked El Charro.

"He has never minded the rain very much," El Charro said, patting the horse gently on his side.

As they walked, it was hard to concentrate on the sounds around them. The rain began to fall harder, and soon Miguel's clothes were drenched. Through the patter of the drops of rain, he thought he heard something, like a small whine in the distance. He looked around at the group, but no one else seemed to have heard it.

When Conde tilted his head up, Miguel knew he was not imagining it. As the rain began to taper off, he heard it again.

"Did you hear that?" Natalia asked.

El Charro kept walking.

"I heard it," Miguel said, moving forward. La Llorona and Death did not seem to hear him, and they continued walking, quickening their pace.

When Miguel heard it again, it was right behind him—a soft cry, like that of a newborn baby. As he made to turn around, Death stopped walking.

"Don't."

El Charro had disappeared, taking the torch with him.

"Don't turn around," La Llorona said softly.

Miguel felt something grabbing at his shoulder, with long, thin, brittle fingers. The claw gripped him tightly, the nails digging into his skin. Suddenly there was a bright light and Miguel felt a sharp pang of heat on his shoulder as the flame from the torch exploded into the air. A sharp wail filled the forest, then all grew quiet. The torch returned to its normal glow, its light dancing on the faces of the others as they turned toward Miguel.

When Miguel looked around, El Charro was standing over a large bird-like creature. Its feathers had been burned badly on one side, its eyes open, having been caught by surprise by the flame.

"What happened?!" Miguel asked, reaching down to hold Conde back from approaching the creature.

"The lechuza," El Charro said. "It never stopped following us."

"But we saw it flying away," Natalia said. "When did it come back?"

"Probably a little bit before the first cry you heard," La

Llorona said, looking down at the creature.

"You heard it too?" Miguel asked, moving closer. The eyes seemed to be following him as he moved.

"Crying, especially the sound of a child crying, is one of the most common ways a lechuza will try to lure someone to their deaths. This one has been following us for some time, and it seems it was given orders to kill us. Or at least, you, Miguel," El Charro said, looking at Miguel with dark red eyes.

Natalia stretched her arm out, offering Miguel a pair of clean, white socks. "Can you tighten them around your shoulder somehow?"

Miguel looked at his shirt, where small trickles of blood had started to fall from the puncture wounds on his shoulder. As he tried to move it, he realized the lechuza's hands had punctured his shoulder quite deeply. He held his shoulder for a moment before taking Natalia's socks and trying to create a makeshift bandage from them.

"Do you think there are others?" he asked as he tied the socks together.

"Yes," Death said, looking into the darkness. "We must hurry. One lechuza is not a problem, but who knows how many creatures have been sent to watch us." Death moved to the back of the group as El Charro resumed his spot at the front.

Miguel reached down and untied the shirt protecting Conde from the rain. Conde lifted his nose in the air, his grey coat glistening with spots of water. A deep, low growl began to form in his throat as he looked into the darkness ahead, his hackles slowly rising and making him look as wild as a wolf. He began to bare his teeth, his sharp canines glistening with the light of the moon. Miguel bent down and caught him as Conde tried to leap forward into the darkness. El Charro's horse reared back, kicking its front legs furiously. El Charro grabbed his reins with his left hand, his right trying to hold the torch forward to look into the darkness.

"Hold him," Death whispered, so close that Miguel almost fell back. Death began to walk forward, his scythe held out in front of him.

El Charro backed away, pulling his horse with him. Soon he and Miguel were side by side, both trying to restrain their friends. Natalia moved back, helping Miguel by grabbing Conde from the back. La Llorona moved forward, following Death toward whatever was coming.

Death stopped walking, moving a hand in front of La Llorona, forcing her to stop.

There was a deep, ugly snarl, and Conde jumped up, trying to escape from Miguel's grip.

Two red eyes moved in the darkness in front of them,

and at first Miguel thought it must be a wolf or a coyote. As the creature approached them, they saw it was almost twice the size of a large dog, its black fur glistening with water from the rain. As the dog walked closer to Death, Miguel saw that its head almost reached Death's shoulder. Death placed his scythe in front of him, and the dog stopped.

It sniffed the air and growled again, and Conde and the horse pulled to get loose.

"Is it…just a dog?" Natalia asked.

"Not just a dog," La Llorona said. "A cadejo."

La Lechuza

THE OWL

ISABEL WAS THE ELDEST of the three daughters, and from a young age she took on responsibilities that her younger sisters did not have to when they grew up. Her grandmother taught her how to sew when she was a little girl, and as she got older she began to save the money she'd made from small sewing jobs to open up her own sewing shop. Her sisters had also learned to sew, and as they grew older, they too showed much talent for the craft.

The sisters often spoke of opening up the shop together. They imagined a wonderful life together as *costureras*, making beautiful dresses and clothing for their patrons.

"What should we name our shop?" the youngest sister, Ana, asked.

"I have the perfect name," the second youngest sister, Sofia, said. "What about, 'The Three Sisters'?

They all nodded in agreement. That was the perfect name.

While out one day without her sisters, Isabel saw a notice advertising a small store space for sale. She knew this would be the perfect place for her and her sisters to set up their shop. She traveled to the bank where she withdrew most of her savings, which she would use to purchase the small store.

She arrived and signed the paperwork, hesitating only slightly as she turned over the money she had worked so hard to save. Isabel decided to surprise the sisters with their new store, so she invited them to accompany her, using the pretext of needing to purchase some items at some of the shops. The sisters were hesitant, pointing out that the sky was growing dark, and heavy clouds were gathering. When they noticed Isabel's urgent expression, they decided to come with her, not wanting her to bear the bad weather alone. As they passed the store, Isabel was ready to reveal to her sisters that she had purchased this beautiful spot with her hard-earned money. All the work she had done throughout the years had finally paid off.

As she arrived at the store, her heart stopped. A large sign hanging over the door read *"Las Tres Hermanas."* The windows were covered in heavy, crimson red curtains, and a sign taped to the glass said BIENVENIDOS.

Isabel rushed up the small steps and pushed the door open. A small chime rang out, and footsteps began to approach from the back of the shop.

"Welcome," a tall woman said, extending her hand to Isabel as she approached.

Isabel pulled back. Her sisters had caught up to her and, startled at her rudeness, stepped forward and extended their own hands.

"Thank you so much," they both said together. "This is a beautiful shop."

"Thank you," the woman said, bowing slightly. "My sisters and I just moved in to this small spot not too long ago. I am Amana, and this is—"

"There must be some mistake," Isabel said sharply. "This is my store. I signed a contract purchasing it only a few days ago." She began to look through her bag. Where was the paper? Where was it? She had placed it in her purse just before they left. She knew her sisters would not believe her when she told them she had purchased the shop. She had brought it along just for that purpose.

"I am so sorry, my dear, there must be some mistake," Amana said. She walked over to the glass counter covered in trinkets. Pulling out a long sheet of paper, she turned it over to show the three sisters. There it was, the contract Isabel had signed. But, instead of her name at the bottom, it held the name of these three sisters: Amana, Catalina, and Marzia.

"No, that can't be," Isabel said. "I signed the papers, I paid the money for this shop." Her voice began to rise.

"I'm so sorry, my dear, but you'll need to lower your voice, or I will have to ask that you please leave the store and return another time," Amana said calmly.

Isabel shook her head. Her sisters grabbed her by the arms, pulling her gently back. "I'll prove it to you," Isabel said, leading her sisters to the bank. When she asked to see her account, her sisters were shocked to see it was almost completely empty.

"Do you see? I paid for it, I paid for that store."

Ana and Sofia looked at one another.

"But, Isabel, this only shows you withdrew the money. It does not show where it went."

Isabel rummaged through her bag, turning it over, the

contents spilling on the floor. As a man passed by in front of them, Isabel recognized him as the man that sold her the store.

"Sir, sir please. Do you remember me? You sold me that spot on the corner only a few days ago. The small shop with the large windows?"

The man looked at her for only a second before answering. "I'm sorry, you must have me mistaken with someone else." Turning, he began to walk away from her.

Isabel ran after him, grabbing at his arm. "No, please, you must remember, I know you do."

Before her sisters caught up to her and pulled her away, the man whispered, "I remember," and winked at her.

Isabel shook her head, realization setting in. She had been swindled.

"Isabel, what is going on?" Ana asked.

"What happened to your money?" Sofia whispered.

Isabel shook her head, not speaking a word until they arrived home. Searching everywhere, she knew she would not find the documents. Something had happened, but, looking at her sisters as they watched her with concern, she knew she would not be able to explain what. She had been cheated.

That night, looking out into the dark sky, Isabel felt an

anger inside of her that felt as if it was bubbling up. She felt herself changing in the moonlight, felt herself grow large wings. As she leaped out of the window, she flew through the sky, vowing to find the man who had taken her possessions.

Ana and Sofia never found out what happened to their sister Isabel. Sometimes, at night, they still hear the sad cry of an owl nearby, not knowing it is their sister coming to visit them.

Twenty-six

AS THE CADEJO BEGAN to circle the group, La Llorona stood in front of them and covered them with her cloak, trying to protect the sides that Death could not reach.

The cadejo growled and began to crouch, as if he was going to try to jump over Death to reach the group.

"You can try," Death said in a low voice.

A shrill whistle came from the distance, and the cadejo's ears shot up. His teeth bared, he looked straight at Miguel and Conde before turning and leaping into the darkness.

Conde was still struggling to break free, and Miguel could feel his heart beating through his chest.

Death turned and walked up to Miguel.

"They sent him," La Llorona said, not asking.

"They did," El Charro said, running his hands softly over his horse's mane.

"For the boy," Death said.

"Death—" La Llorona began.

"I am assuming you have figured out what it is your grandfather left for you to fight the vampire?"

Miguel stepped back, caught off guard. "Yes," he said after a few moments.

Death nodded. "That's why they came for him."

"For me?" Miguel asked.

Death turned to him. "Why else would they send a lechuza and a cadejo to watch us? A black cadejo, who cannot be killed except by a white cadejo? Why would they do that unless they were afraid?"

"Then why did they leave me alive?" Miguel asked, his heart racing.

"They were called back," La Llorona said uncertainly. "Who knows why?"

"We must be very careful, and we must hurry," Death said, looking toward each of them in turn. "Miguel, keep your grandfather's answer close. Natalia, do not worry, we will find your brother. Let us hope there are not many more cadejos in their service."

"More of those dogs?" Natalia said, visibly shaking. "There are more of them?"

"How many do you think they have?" El Charro asked, looking around into the forest.

Death shook his head. "Cadejos are often found alone, but this one is working for the tlahuelpuchi. If one has allied itself with a vampire, who is to say there are not others?"

Miguel looked down at Conde hopelessly, wondering how they were going to be able to get through this. How were they supposed to get past a dog that large? More importantly, how were they supposed to defeat the creature that controlled it? And what if Death was right, what if there were more cadejos? And none of them knew how many tlahuelpocmimi they were going to have to face. Was it just the one who took Benjamín? Miguel reached up, passing the palm of his hand over his forehead, which had begun to throb. The moon had moved in the sky, and its light became blinding. Why did he come here? Why hadn't he just stayed in his grandfather's house with Conde? At least there he could have been happy. What was he doing in this forest? Why did his grandfather have to leave? What was he thinking coming on this trip? None of this was real. Miguel shook his head. This was not happening.

He placed his face in his hands and, on his knees, he felt like looking up at the sky and howling at the moon. He felt like howling until there was no more voice, until there was no more breath and no more life in him. But instead, he just held his face in his hands, trying not to cry. How could something so horrible have happened? How could his grandfather be gone? The whole trip, when his mind tried to go back to his last days with Abuelo, he had pushed the memories away. He kept walking, kept watching Natalia, wondering how she could keep going, how the world could keep going? Any time his brain tried to register that this was real, he pushed the thoughts away, not allowing them to be accepted. But now, as the visions of his grandfather on the porch and as the warmth of Abuelo's skin under his hand came to him, he could not push anything away. The nausea in his stomach traveled up to his throat, and he had to force himself to swallow everything back. But still he shook his head. Because this wasn't happening, this couldn't be happening. It was impossible. He was not going to go through his life without his grandfather, because that life would never be as happy as it could have been.

Natalia placed a hand on his shoulder. "Miguel, are you okay?" she asked, her voice soft.

Miguel did not want to take his hands away from his face. He wanted to ask one of them to take him and Conde home, to take them back so they could leave this behind and forget everything.

"I'm fine," he finally said.

"Are you sure?" she asked. Reaching over, she tried to

pull his hands gently from his face.

Miguel stood, uncovering his face.

"I'm fine," he said, his voice sharp.

Natalia pulled her hands back toward her chest, wincing. After a few moments, she walked toward him. "Miguel, I understand—" she began.

"Understand what?" Miguel asked.

"It's very hard, this is all very hard, for all of us. I understand. I know you miss your grandfather, and I'm so sorry."

As La Llorona began to walk toward him, El Charro tried to reach over and pull her back.

"Miguel," she said, "we understand. Sometimes grief—"

Miguel felt a sharp pain in his chest. "You understand?" He shook his head. "You can't understand. You're not even real."

"Miguel!" Natalia said, her voice rising.

"She's not real. They're not real," Miguel said as he pointed at each of them. "This is not real, Natalia. None of it is."

"Then what is it, Miguel? Your imagination? Your imagination just created this fictitious world where my brother gets kidnapped? What about your grandfather? Miguel, you cannot ignore this, and you cannot use the supernatural to pretend that none of this is real. You cannot hide behind it to ignore your grandfather's death."

It felt as if a hundred metal blades were twisting and turning in Miguel's chest, trying to pull themselves out but instead embedding even deeper in his heart.

"I think you should try to calm down." El Charro's voice was steady. "The forest takes advantage of the darkness inside you to—"

"The darkness inside of me? What about the darkness inside each of you?"

"Miguel, please," La Llorona said. "We must not waste any time. We must hurry to get to Natalia's brother."

"Go then! Just go! Conde and I will find our way out of this place. I'm sure as soon as you're all gone I'll wake up." Miguel's voice sounded weak, even to him. This couldn't be real.

"We are wasting time," La Llorona said, the kindness leaving her voice.

Miguel turned away from them, closing his eyes. "This isn't real, none of it. None of you are real." His voice grew louder as he spoke. He turned around, opening his eyes again. As he looked at each of them he spoke, his voice cold and dark. "You are just a crazy woman, you are just some wandering mariachi that travels with his horse, and you're—"

"That's enough!" El Charro said, stepping forward, his

eyes flaming red.

"No, let him finish," Death said, stepping forward, his voice hollow. "I'm what?"

"You're—you're nothing. You're just the hooded grim reaper from movies and books, and that's why my mind conjured you up so easily."

El Charro stepped back, holding on to his horse's reins, the fire in his eyes growing dark. La Llorona moved slowly, placing her arm carefully in front of Natalia, who was staring, her eyes wide.

"This isn't real, none of this is real," Miguel repeated.

When Death spoke, his voice was hard. "I know you don't want to believe your grandfather has passed away, Miguel, but he has. This *is* real. I wish it wasn't. I wish he was here instead of you, because then we wouldn't be wasting so much time. You may be your grandfather's grandson, but you are nothing like him."

The moments of silence that followed seemed endless.

Miguel hesitated before lifting his face to look at Death. He walked a few steps, but even his footsteps were silent. He shook his head. "This isn't real."

"Have you ever considered that you are not the only person on this journey who has lost someone? That, in fact, there is no one on this journey that has not experienced loss."

Miguel swallowed. "It doesn't matter."

"Doesn't it? Does it not matter that, while you are experiencing this journey in regret and sadness, your friend Natalia sees her brother closer than ever?"

"That's different," Miguel began.

"What is? The way your grandfather passed away in your presence, while she is not sure what her brother has been experiencing?"

"Why are you telling me this?"

"Because, if your grandfather were here, he would tell you the same thing. He was an old man. He was ready to go."

"You don't know that! You don't know him!"

"I..." Death began, then stopped. "He was not afraid, and he had no regrets. You must know that is true."

Miguel stayed silent. Looking around, it seemed as if El Charro and La Llorona were not breathing.

"Take this as your first and final warning. Begin to appreciate life and death as your grandfather did."

"Appreciate? My grandfather was not supposed to die yet. He was a good person, he was healthy, he didn't do anything wrong. What is there to appreciate about a life that is so unfair and a death that comes too quickly?"

Natalia covered her mouth with her hands. La Llorona turned away, not wanting to look at Miguel.

"Your grandfather did not think that way," Death said.

"Why did you take him? Why did you take him?" Miguel's voice was desperate.

"Miguel, your grandfather was ready. His only regret was leaving you. Perhaps he knew you still had not learned something very important."

"And what is that?"

"You see things in black and white. Good and bad. You think that because people are good, they should not die." Death sighed. "I have been in this world for a very long time. Too long, I think. I meet many people on their journey to the lands that wait beyond. Some of them, like your grandfather, are ready to go. Others are not. They even try to bribe me, can you believe it?" Death chuckled. "Here, on this Earth, people are separated by class, by riches. Death makes no such distinction. Your grandfather knew this. Take this as your final warning. Live your life in such a way so that when we meet again, you will not beg me for it."

"Then why not take me now?" Miguel choked. "Why not take me now, so that I can be with my grandfather?"

Death stayed silent for several long moments. He sighed. When he spoke again, his voice was barely above a whisper.

"Are you so sure that you would be going to the place where your grandfather went?"

Miguel's breath caught in his throat.

Death's voice was distant as he continued. "Miguel, you may feel as if you have lost your heart, but try to understand what your grandfather would feel upon seeing you again. How would he feel knowing you were not part of this world anymore?" Death paused before continuing. "And how would he feel to know you were so afraid to live in this world without him?"

Miguel closed his eyes, trying to imagine seeing Abuelo again.

"Knowing that your children—or grandchildren—have lost their life is more unbearable than any pain," La Llorona said, looking at Miguel, her eyes dark green.

El Charro turned away, hiding his face in the shadows.

"Now," Death said, moving to look beyond a group of trees. "We cannot afford to waste any more time. So, whoever you are, show yourself."

Natalia turned her gaze toward the trees that were shrouded in darkness in time to see a small person emerge, their clothes torn and their face full of scratches.

El Charro stepped forward, his eyes blazing red. "It's the chaneque."

Twenty-seven

T HE CHANEQUE STEPPED FORWARD carefully, watching El Charro with its small black eyes.

"Is this the one you were following in Guanajuato?" La Llorona asked.

"And I would have caught him, too, if you had not interrupted me," El Charro said with a slight smile.

The chaneque lifted its hand slightly in greeting.

"Please, I come to help," he said softly. His voice was so low Natalia had to lean in to hear him. She noticed his beige pants and shirt were torn at the knees and elbows, and he was not wearing any shoes. His ears were slightly pointed, and there was a small vine of leaves around the collar of his shirt.

"Go on," Death said.

"I—my name is Adumbral. I come from a family of chaneques that live in Guanajuato. That is where you," he nodded toward El Charro, "were trying to catch me."

El Charro nodded, his eyebrow raised, waiting for Adumbral to continue.

"I have come to help you find the home of the tlahuelpuchi."

Natalia smiled, her eyes crinkling. She wished Benjamín were here.

La Llorona stepped forward. "How do we know you are not working for the tlahuelpuchi? How do we know you are telling the truth?"

Adumbral was quiet, then he looked up at La Llorona. "You do not. There is no way to know. But this girl's brother, the small boy Benjamín, his blood is to be taken before the sun rises. So, you must trust me."

La Llorona looked at El Charro. "Your family… some of them have joined with the tlahuelpuchi. It is very hard for us to trust you."

Adumbral looked down at the ground, his hands clasped together. "I am not like them."

"And you know how to get us to the tlahuelpuchi?" Death asked, stepping close.

Adumbral stepped back. "Yes. I know." He looked up at

Death, his eyes wide with fear. But his voice did not tremble.

"Then we will follow you," Death said. "Lead the way."

Adumbral nodded once, before turning and breaking into a run. "Please, you must run," he said, already panting.

They ran through the trees, not turning when they heard a soft hoot, not wanting to know whether it was really an owl or not.

Natalia ran ahead, trying to catch up to Adumbral. "So, what are you doing out here?" she asked, curious.

"And does your family know what you are doing?" El Charro asked.

Adumbral looked back at them, but continued running. His little feet almost seemed to fly over the trees. Miguel remembered what his grandfather had told him: chaneques and duendes for the most part did no harm, and while some lived in homes, others lived in forests, among the trees. It was clear Adumbral was comfortable with the trees, moving so quickly in the dark.

"My family does not know," Adumbral answered. "My family… they do not speak to me anymore."

"Why is that?" La Llorona asked.

"My family moved here to join the tlahuelpuchi, along with many other creatures—"

"What creatures?" El Charro asked.

"Terrible, dark creatures. Creatures from nightmares. Evil lechuzas, cadejos, and other duendes and chaneques that have joined the dark side."

"What is happening?" El Charro asked, his voice rising. "Why are they joining together?"

"My family said you were very clever," Adumbral told him. "They said you were quick to figure that out."

"What?" La Llorona asked.

"Something is happening," Adumbral said, looking back quickly. "I do not know what it is. When my family joined the tlahuelpuchi, we were promised protection, we were promised great things. My family accepted it. They agreed that the humans had reigned too long over this world. The creatures began to act strange, making pacts with one another when usually they would never talk. When I told them it was wrong, wrong to join them and wrong to help take the children, they told me to leave and never come back." Adumbral cleared his throat. "I stayed close by, trying to help the children they brought. I heard whispers that you were near, trying to rescue the small boy, and that there was a man with red eyes, and I knew it was the man looking for me in the forest. I knew you would help get the boy out safely."

Natalia shifted her backpack to her left shoulder, trying to relieve some of the strain. Miguel listened to their voices, to the screeches in the distance that had suddenly gotten louder, to Conde's panting and steady footfalls, to the rustling of Death's cloak, and to the pounding of his own heartbeat. He looked up at the sky. Only a few short hours and the sun would rise. He shifted his own backpack, wondering whether he should leave it altogether.

"We are not too far," Adumbral said after a long silence. "I am afraid I will not be able to go inside with you. My family has banished me, and I cannot enter."

"Then I will be in good company," Death said.

Natalia looked over at Death in alarm. "You will not enter with us?"

"I cannot," Death said. "I cannot enter a dwelling unless I am invited."

"Invited?" Natalia asked.

"He means—" La Llorona began, but Adumbral had stopped running. He crouched down behind a pile of fallen trees, motioning for them to join him. Hidden behind the trees, they could see a large clearing with a small lake. A beige, two-story stucco house with a red tiled roof and small balcony stood next to the lake, and a silver two-door sports car was parked near the fountain at the entrance.

"This is the place?" Miguel asked in disbelief.

"What, did you expect a towering castle?" Natalia said, looking over at him and attempting to laugh.

Miguel smiled back at her. He could almost feel her heart beating through her chest.

"To be honest, I did."

El Charro laughed. "Get with the times, Miguel."

Adumbral turned to look at them. "You must be very careful. Pay close attention. There are two stories in this house, and two stairways, one leading to the left, and another leading to the right. The children are kept in one of the rooms upstairs. I do not know how many tlahuelpocmimi there are now, but there were at least three the last time I checked. There are also two lechuzas, and four cadejos."

"Is that all?" El Charro asked, his eyes wide.

"And the chaneques," Adumbral said quietly. "But I will take care of them." He stood up, getting ready to run into the woods again. Turning to Miguel, he stepped closer. "Miguel, the tlahuelpuchi knows you have in your possession a weapon that can defeat her. You must listen very carefully."

Miguel leaned in, swallowing hard.

"The tlahuelpuchi must drink it."

Miguel's eyes widened. An image of the tiny bottle in his backpack flashed through his mind. Drink it? How in the world was he supposed to get three grown vampires to drink that?

"How do you know that?" Miguel asked.

"Your grandfather, he told me they must drink it."

"How do we get in the house?" La Llorona asked.

"There…" Adumbral hesitated, "there is no way for you to enter undetected."

"What?" El Charro asked.

"They already know you are here." Adumbral looked up at them, and for a moment the moon came out from behind the clouds and his eyes brightened. Miguel saw the black swirls inside his brown eyes, the loneliness.

"Thank you for bringing us here," Miguel said, thinking of something his grandfather might say.

Adumbral nodded. "I know you can do it. You will not let the darkness win." He turned and began to run.

"But wait!" Natalia said. "How will we know where to find you?"

"Find me?" Adumbral stopped, "For what?"

"Well, to see that you're okay?"

"To see that I'm okay?" Adumbral smiled. "I will be okay. Good luck to you in finding your brother." He looked at Miguel. "And good luck to you, for your grandfather."

Miguel's eyes widened.

Adumbral cleared his throat. "I gave him a message, that the tlahuelpuchi was coming. He believed me. Thank you for believing me too. You look much like him, young

Miguel."

Before Miguel had a chance to respond, Adumbral turned and disappeared into the night.

El Charro and La Llorona looked at each other, and then at Death.

"Do not tell me you are afraid," Death said. "Come, if a small creature like that can have such courage, surely we can as well."

Miguel had not realized he was holding on to Conde so tightly. Conde looked up at him and, for a brief moment, Miguel thought that he was smiling. It occurred to him that Death sounded like he was smiling too.

And why not? They would find Benjamín and destroy the tlahuelpuchi.

"Well, what are we waiting for?" Miguel said.

Death nodded. "That's the spirit, Abraham."

Death began to walk toward the house, his scythe held close to his body. Miguel watched him, wondering if Death realized what he had just said.

Twenty-eight

THE WOODEN DOORS WERE large and, from what Miguel could tell, very heavy. If they were not open, they were going to have a difficult time getting inside. Death stood off to the right of the porch, shrouded in shadows.

"Will you be okay?" Natalia asked him.

"He'll be fine," La Llorona said, rolling her eyes and laughing.

If Miguel squinted his eyes a little bit, he could almost believe they were a group of teenagers trick or treating, waiting for someone to answer the door. He chuckled.

El Charro and La Llorona looked back at him, and Miguel's face reddened.

"Stay close," La Llorona said to them, and Natalia and

Miguel nodded.

"Stay behind us," El Charro added.

"I think one of you will need to open the door," La Llorona said. Natalia stepped forward, anxious to get inside. She turned the gold knob and there was a slight *click*. Miguel held his breath. Of course it was open. The vampires wanted them to come inside.

Conde's fur began to rise up, his eyes bright and sharp, his ears raised. Miguel bent down and held him close, breathing in the smell of his warm fur. It felt like Conde was the last remaining piece of his grandfather, and for a moment, it was as if Miguel's grandfather was there. Miguel reached into his backpack pouch and pulled out his rolled-up socks, the small chain falling into his palm. He placed it gently in his pocket, put the socks into his backpack, and placed the pack on the floor. It would only slow him down.

As they stepped inside the house, there was a cold burst of air mixed with a deep humid scent. A small wooden table stood in the entryway, a vase of purple Mexican petunias on top. Gold ornate sconces lined a small hall that led into a large entry room. A plush gold and red carpet muffled their footsteps as they walked inside, Miguel closing the door gently behind him. El Charro had insisted his horse walk behind Miguel, assuring them that the horse would be able to warn him of any danger that was approaching.

At the far end of the room, just as Adumbral had said, there were two large wooden staircases, one leading to the right, the other to the left, meeting in the middle in a V shape. They stopped in the center of a large room and looked around. Natalia continued walking toward the staircases, but La Llorona pulled her back.

"We must be careful. We do not know which staircase is the one that leads to the children."

Natalia stopped walking, but Miguel could tell it was taking all her strength to hold herself back. Her fingers were trembling as she rubbed her hands together, but Miguel knew she was not afraid.

The light from the candles gave off a soft, warm glow, so that, if they did not know this was the home of a vampire, they could have believed that it was the house of a good friend, and this was simply a nice night to get together for dinner.

The carpet had stopped at the entryway door, the floor in this room a dark brown wood. Gilded frame portraits hung on the walls—a family portrait with a man and woman and their two children, one of a young woman in a dark red dress, and another of a young man in a white suit. Miguel's breath caught as he realized who it was, the doctor's eyes watching him closely even now. Miguel absently began to walk toward the portrait, trying to get a closer look at the eyes.

Natalia looked up at the staircases, wondering which one would lead her to the room Benjamín was in. She closed her eyes for a moment, thinking of her brother's silly crooked smile whenever they made smores in the microwave or when he convinced her to look at his comics underneath his blanket. Her throat tightened and her eyes burned thinking of what might be happening, what might have happened to him as he waited all this time.

"I'm coming, Benjamín," she whispered.

She moved a few steps closer to Miguel, looking at the portraits on the wall. The young woman in the red dress was smiling slightly, almost as if the artist had asked her to and that was the only bit of smile she could muster. Her skin was pale and stiff, and the dark brown—almost black—eyes were filled with something Natalia could not describe.

Conde was sniffing the ground slowly, his nose going over every spot on the floor. In the flickering candlelight, some of his fur looked almost gold. El Charro and La Llorona's heads were bent together, whispering, undoubtedly discussing which way to go. There was an arched doorway to their left and their right, and from what they could see with the candlelight on the walls, the hallways were narrow and each had a closed door at the end. And straight ahead, in between the V formed by the staircases, was a large double door with heavy brass doorknobs.

"Should we go upstairs?" Natalia asked, her voice trembling slightly. Miguel knew if they waited any longer Natalia would go upstairs with or without them.

Conde stopped walking and stood between Natalia and Miguel, reaching his paw up to scratch Miguel in the leg. Miguel looked down at his wide eyes and the white hairs on his chin. He bent down on one knee and pulled him close, feeling Conde's heartbeat. It was steady.

Conde rested his chin on Miguel's shoulder, and for a moment Miguel could smell in the air a mixture of Conde's soft fur and his grandfather's warm clothes after they were hung to dry. As Conde pulled away, Miguel could see his smile in his eyes.

"It's going to be all right," Natalia said, looking at Conde. "I think he knows it's going to be all right."

Miguel nodded, but for some reason his chest felt as if it was tightening, as if the air was thinning and there was not enough.

El Charro's horse reared up as Conde's hackles stood on end, his ears pointed up straight. He looked up at Miguel and Natalia, his eyes bright and ready, before turning toward the stairs. He walked forward a few paces, and as the light flickered on his fur, Miguel could almost swear Conde looked like a gray wolf in the light of the moon.

"Something is coming," El Charro said, pulling his horse back. There was a low rumble, and La Llorona turned her head toward the door to the left, then to the right, unsure of where the noise was coming from.

"Stay behind us," she said in a low voice.

A snarl came from the left, and Miguel's heart sank as he realized what was coming.

Before Miguel could reach him, Conde leapt forward, landing ahead of El Charro and his horse. As Miguel ran to grab him, a snarl came from the door on the right where he and Natalia were standing. Two large black cadejos walked into the room, separating Natalia and Miguel from the others. Another snarl came from the left, and two more cadejos walked in slowly. As El Charro struggled to pull his horse back, his boots slipped and he fell backward, his horse pulling free. He reared back, kicking his front legs toward the cadejos, who backed away, but only for a moment. As they locked eyes on Miguel, they began to move to the other side of the room to join the other two, who were closing in on Natalia. As La Llorona turned to shield them, El Charro pulled her back.

Conde turned, his teeth bared, and released a long, low growl. The cadejos turned and locked eyes with him, and for a moment no one moved. Miguel's voice was strangled in his throat, his heart pounding. He ran forward, but Natalia pulled him back with all her strength and they fell back on the floor together.

Conde was backing away toward the door on the left, and Miguel realized what he was doing. For a moment he was back at his grandfather's house, back in the room after his grandfather had left him, not wanting to believe what was happening. But it was real. And this time he knew it.

Conde looked at him for one long moment, his eyes softening as they met Miguel's. Miguel saw him running with the piglets in his grandfather's ranch, saw him carrying Amelia when she was a baby, saw him laying side by side with Miguel as they watched caterpillars walking in the grass. Conde's big, bright eyes lingered on Miguel's for a moment longer, a steady gaze that never wavered. Miguel saw once more that his grandfather was right—you can tell a lot through someone's eyes.

Conde turned his eyes, sharp and ready, to the cadejos, and let out one low, deep growl. As the cadejos all leapt toward him, Conde turned and ran through the hallway on the left, the snarls echoing down the hall. Miguel ran after him, El Charro pushing him to the ground as the growls and snarls reached the end of the hall.

"No!" Miguel screamed. "No! Please no! Anything but that!"

"Miguel, those creatures were sent to kill you. We have

to protect you," La Llorona said.

"I have to help him! I can't lose him, not him too!"

There was a loud yelp, and then everything was silent.

Miguel pushed El Charro off with all his strength, howling with all the breath in his lungs. Standing, he ran toward the hallway as the four cadejos reached the door. Their eyes locked on Miguel, their teeth stained with blood. Miguel felt the heat growing in his hands as he threw himself toward the cadejos, an anger like he had never felt before crawling up his throat, strangling him.

The cadejos leapt toward him as a strong wind threw Miguel back through the air, pushing him into the wooden floor. A black shadow moved in front of him, silver glinting in the candlelight. Death stood in front of them, blocking the path to the cadejos. Their eyes shifted from Miguel to Death and back, the growls in their throat deep and long. Death raised his scythe into the air, bringing it down with such force that cracks appeared in the wood floor. "Not today," he said.

Howls began to fill the air, and a soft wind came in from the doorways. The black cadejos raised their ears, their eyes uncertain. As they bent down, getting ready to attack, four large white dogs flew over Miguel, landing next to Death. He lifted his scythe and brought it down once more as the black cadejos leapt in the air, the white cadejos meeting them halfway. The black cadejos fell to the ground, their throats torn and bloody, and quickly turned and ran through the archway, the white cadejos close behind. There was a loud crash as they reached another room in the house, and then, silence.

Natalia bent down, pulling Miguel up. Miguel looked around the room and at the floor, anywhere but in her eyes.

Death stood silently near the doorway, waiting to see if the black cadejos would return.

"Is he gone?" Miguel asked, walking up to Death. "Is Conde gone?"

Death did not turn away from the door. "Yes."

"Are you sure?" Miguel asked, his voice pleading.

Death lowered his head, looking toward the ground.

"I would not be here if he wasn't."

Twenty-nine

A HIGH-PITCHED VOICE broke the silence. "Natalia, Natalia, is that you?" Natalia turned up toward the stairs. Benjamín stood at the top of the staircase on the right, his clothes dirty and tattered.

"Benjamín!" Natalia said, running toward the stairs. La Llorona pulled her back. "Natalia, wait."

"It's him! It's him!" Natalia said, pulling away. Benjamín turned and ran up the rest of the stairs and into the hallway to the right, Natalia leaping over the steps two at time. La Llorona flew after her, both of them disappearing through the doorway.

As Miguel watched, the large double doors opened up in front of them. El Charro's horse began to whinny and pull back as three women walked in through the doorway.

Death stiffened.

"Natalia! Is that you?" the woman on the left mocked.

El Charro stepped back so he and Miguel were now side by side.

"Watch yourself, Miguel. Tlahuelpocmimi are very fast, and very clever."

"I'm surprised you're still alive, boy," the woman on the right said to Miguel.

"That must have been your doing," the woman on the left spat at Death.

Death moved forward slowly.

The woman in the middle still had not spoken. She wore a black suit and red leather jacket, and Miguel realized she was the girl from the portrait. Was she the doctor's sister? Was she the tlahuelpuchi that had killed his grandfather?

"Yes, too bad they couldn't come in time to save the boy's dog," the one on the right laughed.

Miguel ran forward without thinking, but a strong wind lifted him up in the air, making him land on the cracked floor with a thud.

Death's dark figure loomed in front of him.

Finally, the woman in the middle spoke. "You've got courage, boy. Just like your grandfather."

Miguel stood again, trying to run forward, but El Charro

pulled him back.

"Not yet, Miguel. You have to wait for the right moment."

Miguel stopped. He felt as if his pocket was burning, almost felt the cold metal of the necklace with the small bottle his grandfather had left him. She had to drink it. He had to get her to drink it.

"Why don't you two run along? Don't you know that everyone that helps this boy dies?"

"You killed the doctor," Miguel said, his voice shaking. "You killed your brother."

The woman sighed. "He knew what would happen if he helped you or your grandfather, but he did it anyway."

"To stop you. What you're doing here, taking children, killing…"

"I only take what I have to—*we* only take what we have to. We are predators, just like wolves, just like lions. But you don't think what they do is wrong."

"They are following their instincts," El Charro said, "but you know what you are doing is wrong, and you continue."

The woman on the left walked forward. The black suit she wore was almost identical to the one worn by the other two women, but hers had a hint of green.

"You're the demon," she said, and Miguel thought he heard a slight quiver in her voice.

"Careful," the woman on the right said. "He eats the hearts of young women."

"How romantic. How long has it been since you've had a woman's heart?"

"My heart only beats for one woman. I don't need anyone else's heart," El Charro said, his voice tinged with sadness.

"Are you still searching for your children too?" She laughed, but her eyes flickered toward the doorway.

El Charro remained silent. His horse tried to move forward restlessly.

"Your children are upstairs too," the woman on the right said, the blue flecks in her suit as bright as her eyes. "Well, what's left of them."

El Charro's complexion began to turn a deep red, the skin on his face tightening around his skull. Miguel could feel a warmth coming from El Charro, his eyes widening as he realized that this time, El Charro's black horse was changing too, transparent skin offering a view of the horse's skeletal structure underneath. In a single movement, El Charro swung himself on his horse, who reared back. The woman on the left began to back away, her eyes widening in panic. El Charro lowered his sombrero over his face, not wanting Miguel to see his eyes. As the woman turned and began to run up the stairs, the woman on the right tried to follow. The horse leaped over the doctor's sister, and Miguel realized that he was flying, his long, skeletal wings taking him easily over the steps and to the top just as the two women ducked through the doorway. El Charro jumped off his horse and the two of them followed the vampires through the hallway.

"It looks like it's just us now," the doctor's sister said.

Death began to back away towards the archway on the left.

"Leaving so soon?" she asked him. "And here I thought you might want to stay and talk for a while."

There was a loud crash from upstairs, and a high-pitched whinny. Miguel hoped El Charro's horse was not having trouble against the two vampires.

"This is not my battle to fight."

"I didn't know Death could feel fear," the tlahuelpuchi said, her voice cold.

"Why should I be afraid?" Death said, his voice just as icy. "The boy will have no trouble with you. He is Abraham's grandson."

"That man was nothing but an old fool, thinking he could find a way to defeat me."

"Is that a tremble in your voice?" Death asked.

"You forget that Abraham is dead," she said, looking at Miguel as she did.

Without another word to her, Death turned to face Miguel. "I will keep Conde safe."

Turning slightly, he paused and looked back at Miguel. "A man who lives life to the fullest is prepared to die at any time."

As he disappeared under the archway, Miguel felt the burning in his pocket once more.

The tlahuelpuchi began to walk toward him, her steps slow and deliberate.

"You don't have to die today, Miguel. Just give me the bottle and you can go free. You can go back to your grandfather's ranch. I will never return to bother you again."

Miguel looked at her face, and then at the portrait. She had not aged at all since it was painted.

"The benefits of immortality," she said, waving her hand at the painting.

"I'd say it's more of a curse," he replied.

The tlahuelpuchi looked at Miguel, her deep brown eyes almost black in the candlelight.

"And what would you know about curses?" she asked, her voice bitter. "What would you know about having to live forever, to be feared and hated for something that is out of your control?"

"Out of your control? It's not out of your control. You can stop taking children any time. You just don't want to."

"I'll die if I do!"

"Then die! At least your soul would be clean, and at least all these innocent children wouldn't have to pay for your life."

"It is easy for someone else to talk, someone who has no idea what it's like. It's either this or death, and you would never understand."

"I understand," Miguel said, beginning to walk opposite her. As they circled each other, Miguel placed his hands casually in his front pockets, his right hand clasping the silver chain. "I understand that you are just afraid."

"Afraid of what?"

"Death. You are afraid of what waits beyond. If you weren't, you would stop taking these children and face your life head-on."

"It's not that easy!" she yelled, so loudly that the candles flickered.

"Your brother did it. He knew what would happen if he helped us, he knew what would happen if he went against you, but he did it anyway. He was not afraid."

"He betrayed our family—he betrayed me—and for what? For the lives of those who will never appreciate it? For your life?"

Miguel hesitated, his heart slowing down. Never had he stopped to consider that the doctor had sacrificed his life in order for Miguel to keep going. But now as she spoke, he realized it was true.

Miguel stepped closer to her, his grip tightening on the small bottle. He would get close enough to her, then uncork the bottle and throw some of the water down her throat.

"Miguel, I will ask you one last time," she said. "Give me the bottle and I will let you walk free."

They stopped walking, and Miguel faced the tlahuelpuchi, who was standing directly underneath her portrait. He could see her name inscribed in an oval name plate at the bottom. Lisanna.

"Why are you doing this?" Miguel asked.

"I need to survive—"

"No, not just that. All of this. Why are all these creatures here? What are you planning?" He stepped forward.

Before Miguel could react, Lisanna flew forward, pushing him up against the opposite wall. As her hand tightened its grip around his neck, Miguel let go of the bottle in his pocket, his hands trying to pull Lisanna's right hand from his neck, but she was impossibly strong.

With her left hand, Lisanna reached into his pocket and pulled out the bottle on the chain.

"You're just as foolish as your grandfather." She swung the bottle in front of her, tightening her grip on his neck even more, his feet dangling in the air.

She lowered her voice, whispering, "Did you know, that foolish old man thought he could trick me. Do you know what's in here?"

Miguel was struggling to breathe, and his eyes were beginning to close.

"Holy water, yes, and some garlic, a little bit of metal. But the true weapon, the deadly part of this water..." she moved her face so close to Miguel's he could feel her breath in his face, "is your grandfather's tears. Because, you see, Miguel, you need the tears of one who has been killed by the tlahuelpuchi in order to truly defeat a tlahuelpuchi."

Miguel felt her nails pierce his neck, felt the blood running down.

Lisanna threw the bottle to the ground, and as it shattered, she let go of Miguel, who fell limp.

"That fool thought he could trick me. He let me kill him, just so that he could collect the tears you needed to defeat me." She laughed bitterly. "It almost worked."

Miguel's eyes closed, he felt so tired. As he drifted off to sleep, Conde came in from the hallway, his soft footsteps making no noise. He stood over Miguel, but Miguel didn't have the strength to reach up and touch him. Conde bent his head down and licked Miguel's forehead gently. Miguel opened his eyes. His vision was blurry, and as lay on his side, he could see a small piece of glass only a few inches from his face. A small drop of water glinted on its surface.

With incredible speed, the tlahuelpuchi turned and flew toward Miguel, a dagger in her hand. As Miguel felt it pierce his chest, he reached over and covered the small shard of glass with his hand.

"What a fool," she whispered. As she began to laugh, Miguel started to laugh with her. Just as she turned to look down at him, he pushed his hand into her mouth, her sharp teeth cutting into his arm. She bit down hard, tearing at his flesh with her teeth, bright blood dripping down on his shirt. But he didn't let go.

The tlahuelpuchi grabbed her neck, her eyes widening. She pulled Miguel's hand from her mouth, spitting out globs of blood, but it was too late.

There was a loud crash as glass broke on the second floor, and footsteps and horse hooves soon followed down the stairs.

Lisanna's skin was turning a dark grey, and she leaned against the wall, holding her face in her hands. As she looked at Miguel, he saw that her eyes were completely black, her hair white. She turned, trying to reach the hallway, but as she took a few steps, she began to sway. When she fell to the floor, she looked up at her portrait, the black eyes staring into her own.

Thirty

MIGUEL COULD SEE EL Charro and his horse standing over him, El Charro kneeling to shake him gently.

La Llorona wrapped her cloak around his arm, her face covered in scratches. Miguel wanted to ask her if she found her children, but he couldn't speak, his throat felt so sore.

As he saw a tiny shadow block the light above him, he knew Benjamín was okay.

Death came and stood over him, his shadow somehow darker than the others'.

"Do something!" Natalia screamed. "Help him!"

"I cannot interfere," Death said quietly.

La Llorona tore a piece of her cloak, placing it over the wound in Miguel's chest.

"You knew," she said quietly. "You knew he was going to die. And you let him."

Death remained silent.

"You knew?" Natalia asked. "You knew?!"

El Charro spoke, his voice hoarse. "An axolotl will only answer the wishes of one who is near death."

Natalia covered her mouth. "No."

Miguel's eyes flickered, but he did not open them. He was standing near Lake Xochimilco, watching the axolotls swim in the water. He felt someone watching him, and as he turned slowly, he knew who it would be. Abuelo was standing near the trees, Conde sitting peacefully next to him.

Miguel walked toward them, afraid his voice would break if he spoke.

"You can save him," La Llorona said in the distance. "You will save him."

"I cannot interfere," Death said.

"You can. And you will."

"But he will—"

"You already knew that," El Charro said. "At least this will give him some time."

"Abuelo," Miguel said, "Conde."

"Miguel," Abuelo said. "I am so proud of you."

Miguel felt the tears fill his eyes. He didn't trust himself to speak.

Someone cleared their throat. Looking up, Miguel saw

that Death was standing next to Abuelo.

"I can only give you a few moments, Miguel. Your grandfather and Conde must be on their way."

Miguel blinked, and Death was gone.

Abuelo walked over and embraced Miguel, holding him close. Miguel wanted to sob, but he knew once he started he would not be able to talk, and he wanted to say so much to his grandfather.

"Abuelo…" Miguel started. What could he say? Out of all the millions of things in his mind, what could he say? *Please don't leave me, please take me with you and Conde.* But he knew that would make his grandfather sad. He rubbed his eyes, knowing that his grandfather would be able to read what was inside of them.

"I love you, Abuelo." Bending down, Miguel hugged Conde, taking in the warm smell of his soft fur. "I love you, Conde. Thank you for saving my life."

Abuelo chuckled.

"Abuelo?"

"Yes, Miguel?"

Miguel wanted to ask him if what Death had said was true, if he really had been ready to go. But instead he said, "Will you and Conde be here when it is my turn to go?"

His grandfather smiled. "Of course we will."

Death cleared his throat again.

With his scythe, he traced an archway in the trees, a path

wide enough for Conde and Abuelo to walk through.

As they turned to look at Miguel one last time, he saw the deep swirls in their eyes, and he hoped they could tell that he loved them more than he could say.

As the clearing closed behind him, Miguel felt a pulsing sensation in his chest. He closed his eyes for a moment, and when he opened them he was lying down, shadows moving above him. He saw Death bent over him, one cloaked hand uncovered. Miguel narrowed his eyes, not wanting Death to know he was looking at his bony hand.

"He should be back to normal in a few hours," Death said, covering his hand again. "Let's just give him some space before we take them home."

As the others moved away, Death kneeled down, inches away from Miguel's face. "Living."

Miguel opened his eyes. "What?"

"I thought you were asleep," Death said.

Miguel's face burned. "What did you say?"

"Your grandfather asked me to tell you. He said he never got to finish. Living. Don't stop living."

Miguel closed his eyes again, thinking of his grandfather and Conde. He hoped when he woke up, he would be back home again, and for once, was grateful they had some of the fastest transportation available.

Epilogue

MIGUEL AND NATALIA WATCHED as Estela looked for Benjamín and Amelia, who had hidden behind some bushes near the back of the yard. Benjamín roared with laughter.

"He is very strong," Miguel said, almost to himself.

Natalia nodded. "Yes."

It had been a few weeks since Benjamín had been found, and the cool October air had finally arrived.

"Does he…talk about it much?" Miguel asked.

Natalia closed her eyes before answering. "Not really. I think he wants to forget, but I hear him tossing and turning in the night. He calls out the names of the other two children who were with him."

"I'm glad they are back with their families," Miguel whispered.

"Me too," Natalia replied. "I imagine they must have the same wounds Benjamín does. Inside and out."

"But they're safe now," Miguel said, attempting a smile.

"Yes," Natalia smiled back, the nervousness in her voice seeming to ask *for how long?*

The sky began to glow as the sun prepared to set. Natalia looked up nervously.

"Come on, Benjamín, it's time to go!"

Benjamín tagged Amelia and Estela as he ran back to the front of the yard. "You're it!" he yelled, getting the last laugh.

Natalia reached down, taking his hand tightly in hers.

"Bye, Miguel," she said, glancing back one last time before she and Benjamín began to walk home.

"Bye," Miguel waved.

"Miguel, are you coming?" Amelia asked. "We are making popcorn."

"In a minute," Miguel said.

"Okay, but we might eat it all," Estela laughed, running inside behind Amelia.

Miguel sat down on the old wooden bench near the front gate, watching the sun go down.

He closed his eyes. *Just for a minute,* he thought.

The hoots of an owl woke him from his sleep. The sun had set, and the red orange colors in the distance reminded Miguel of the fires his grandfather would make when they were telling stories. He could see his dad through the kitchen window, listening to Antonio Aguilar songs on the radio.

"Those are the classics," a voice next to him said, and Miguel jumped up, startled.

El Charro sat next to him, his horse's reins tied to the fence.

Miguel sat back down, trying to slow the thud of his heart with deep breaths.

"You could give a little bit more warning if you're going to drop by, just saying."

"Surprise is the spice of life, Miguel," El Charro laughed.

Miguel noticed his suit was dusty around the knees, and needed to be mended in some spots.

"Does your horse want some carrots or an apple?"

El Charro laughed a little nervously. "No, he doesn't eat that."

Miguel's eyes widened. "Don't tell me he eats hearts, too? Female horse hearts?!"

"Okay, that's pretty ridiculous, Miguel." El Charro rolled his eyes.

Miguel shook his head.

"He really likes chocolate."

"You're kidding, right?"

El Charro shook his head. "I wish I was."

Miguel raised his eyebrows, trying not to laugh.

El Charro squinted, looking into the kitchen. "Is that your dad?"

Miguel nodded.

"His eyes look familiar," El Charro said.

Miguel looked at his dad. He squinted to get a better look. They did look familiar, like someone he had seen recently.

Miguel shrugged.

"Would you like something?" Miguel asked, not knowing what to offer him.

El Charro remained quiet, petting his horse.

"His name is Mazapan," El Charro said finally.

"That's a nice name," Miguel said, thinking of the candies.

Miguel walked over to the horse, petting him gently. The horse moved slightly, then was still.

"You have a good touch," El Charro said.

He looked at Miguel, his red eyes flickering orange and yellow like the setting sky, then looked back at his horse.

"Can I get you anything?" Miguel asked again.

"No...I just wanted to stop by. I see that you are doing

well."

Miguel nodded, an uneasy feeling pulling at the wound on his chest.

"I'd better go," Miguel said, looking around, not sure if anyone watching could actually see El Charro.

El Charro nodded.

As Miguel walked away, he heard El Charro following him.

"Miguel, wait."

El Charro pulled off his sombrero, scratching his head.

"Miguel…" He hesitated. He looked up, his eyes meeting Miguel's. The oranges and yellows were gone, replaced by dark reds and blacks. He took a deep breath before he spoke.

"Miguel, I need a favor."

Glossary

ALEBRIJE—alebrijes are colorful and fantastical creatures, such as a horse with wings and horns or a lion with a rooster's head, that help to vanquish nightmares. The history and creation of the Alebrije can be traced back to Pedro Linares López, a talented Mexican artisan greatly skilled in the area of cartonería, or papier-mâché. Señor López fell very ill and, in a dream, creatures of all types and colors appeared to him, saying "Alebrijes!" When Don Pedro woke from his dream, he began to use his talents to create the Alebrijes that had come to him in his dream. Alebrijes are still created today, many beautiful creatures of all colors, and having an Alebrije will help to get rid of the nightmares that may be haunting you.

AXOLOTL—a neotenic salamander that has a fin, external gills, and legs, and maintains these features throughout its life. Found now only in Lake Xochimilco in Mexico City, the axolotl was also previously found in Lake Chalco. Due to pollution, the shrinking of Lake Xochimilco, and the introduction of non-native species, the axolotl is now critically endangered and almost impossible to find in the wild. The axolotl has the ability to regenerate limbs completely, and can live up to fifteen years

BIEN—good

CADEJO/HELLHOUND—a large, often black, supernatural dog whose job it sometimes is to take persons down into the underworld. The Cadejo is similar to the hellhound and is often found in folklore of parts of Mexico and Central America. The black Cadejo sometimes has red eyes and is thought to bring bad luck or death. In some legends, the black Cadejo is purely evil. The white Cadejo is the opposite of the black Cadejo; it has a good nature and will protect travelers who need it

CANDIL—oil lamp

CARTONERÍA—papier-mâché

CHANEQUE—little creatures, often associated with nature, similar to sprites or elves who often play tricks on people but cause no real harm

CHARRO—a traditional Mexican horseman

CHICLE—gum

CONDE—Count

COSTURERA—seamstress

DUENDE—elf or goblin

GALLO—rooster

HACIENDA—an estate

LECHUZA—a large creature resembling a screech owl whose screech is said to be an omen of bad luck. Lechuzas are often thought to take the forms of birds and owls. Some legends say that the lechuza will only attack or harm a person who has done wrong. Other legends say that lechuzas were once women who suffered through a terrible unfairness in their lives, and now travel the world in search of revenge. Lechuzas are not often believed to be evil, and are seen as spirits who are warning of forthcoming bad luck, or who cause some misfortune themselves

LEYENDA—legend

MECEDORA—rocking chair

MIS HIJOS—my children

MUY BIEN—very good

NEOTENIC—in axolotls, retaining its larval characteristics

SOMBRERO—a wide-brimmed hat, part of traditional charro dress

SUSTO—shock, scare

XOLOTL—an Aztec god associated with lightning, death, misfortune, and bad luck. Depicted often as a dog or a skeleton with a dog's head, he is often shown to have feet that are backwards. Xolotl is the twin brother of Quetzalcoatl, the feathered serpent, and along with his brother, traveled to the underworld to retrieve bones of the dead to create new life, which has continued on to the present time. During one occasion, when gods were being sacrificed, Xolotl transformed himself into the creature we now know as the axolotl to escape this sacrifice. The axolotl is named after the god Xolotl. Xolotl appears at night and is also believed to guide those who have passed on in their journey to the lands that wait beyond.

Acknowledgments

FOR MY FAMILY:

My mom and dad, who have always worked so hard, and without whom I would be nowhere.

My sisters, who are beautiful and brilliant and have shown me that when you want to do something, you go and do it.

My nieces Melody and Emily, I am so lucky to be the aunt of two such kind, good-natured, clever, beautiful, and witty young women.

My husband Manuel and our dogs, Manchas, Moxie, and Umbra, thank you for showing me every day that everything is meant to be loved and cared for while there is still time; thank you for lighting up my life and my soul with your smiles and your laughter; Manuel, I'm even willing to ignore that they love you more than me.

Lisa and Elizabeth, thank you for listening and for your steadfast friendship, for believing in this book and for thinking my ideas were not crazy. I cannot tell you how grateful I am for your friendship, I breathe easier knowing that I am lucky enough to be able to count on you.

Debbie and Lindsay, thank you for filling so much of my life full of happiness and laughter. I miss you more than you'll ever know, and I can't tell you how much I admire you and how grateful I am that you are part of my life.

Michelle and Veronica, thank you for your constant friendship, words of encouragement, and for bringing so much laughter into my life. I can't tell you how lucky I am that I met you.

About the Author

SELENIA PAZ spends a lot of her time working at a library surrounded by awesome books, and uses the rest of her time to read, write, and run with her dogs. She finds inspiration in everything from history to science and especially loves magical realism. Her manuscript "Broken English" was selected as a 2012 New Voices Honor winner by Lee and Low Books. She is also the author of the short stories "Lisbeth" (*Perchance to Dream: Classic Tales from the Bard's World in New Skins*, 2015), "The Inventor's Daughter (*Magic at Midnight: A YA Fairy Tale Anthology*, 2018) and "The Alchemist's Daughter" (*Brave New Girls: Tales of Heroines Who Hack*, 2018). You can find her online at seleniapaz.com.

Made in the USA
San Bernardino, CA
28 September 2018